Murder in the Napa Valley

A
Margaret
Barlow
Mystery

DAVID
OSBORN

SIMON & SCHUSTER
New York
London
Toronto
Sydney
Tokyo

Insert   Simon & Schuster
S&S   Rockefeller Center
Logo   1230 Avenue of the Americas
           New York, NY 10020

Simon & Schuster and colophon are registered trademarks
   of Simon & Schuster, Inc.

Designed by Deidre C. Anthor

Manufactured in the United States of America

10 9 8 7 6 5 4 3 2 1

Library of Congress Cataloging-In-Publication Data
Osborn, David, date
Murder in the Napa Valley/David Osborn.
p.   cm
"A Margaret Barlow mystery."
1.   Women detectives-California-Napa River Valley-Fiction.
I. Title
PS3565.S37M78   1993
813'.54-dc20   92-47375
CIP
ISBN 0-7432-1294-0

For Robin, Raphaella, and Sebastian

Prologue

THE MEXICAN WAS no longer young and he walked as rapidly as his tired legs could carry him, thin shoulders hunched into the cold night fog that had begun, as it did every night, to pour up the Napa Valley. The narrow road on which he'd come down from the vineyard in the hills was pitch-dark. Twice he'd stumbled off it into the ditch. But soon, he knew, he'd hit the main highway that went south down through the valley, and there'd be traffic and the lights of cars and he'd at least be able to see.

His name was Julio Garcia-Sanchez. With a hundred other migrant agricultural workers, and with papers provided by the United Farm Workers, he'd come the month before all the way from Guadalajara, first by rail to the border at Mexicali, then by truck to Fresno in the Central Valley where he had hoed lettuce for two weeks. Then up to St. Helena in the Napa Valley north of San Francisco, where he and a crew were organized by a local work boss for harvesting grapes in the vineyards.

First he'd picked down in the valley. The work was backbreaking. It began at five in the morning, the men moving slowly through the chill dawn fog between the long rows

of vines. Using a special vineyard knife with a curved ser-
rated blade, they cut away the bunches of grapes from beneath their shelter of leaves and threw them into yellow
plastic bins to be emptied in turn into tractor-towed gondolas
and taken to the winery. There, the grapes were dumped
into the crusher-stemmer that stripped away the leaves and
stalks and crushed them. The work stopped when it got too
dark to see but he was glad to get it.

After a week, his crew moved to one of the vineyards in
the hills above the valley. And now he was leaving, running
away, actually. The crew boss told him if he left he wouldn't
get another job but he didn't care. He had to go. He knew
that. He had to go because of what had happened two years
ago when he'd picked grapes in the same vineyard. The
weather, then, had been cold and the dormitory the men
slept in was unheated and the blanket they'd given him
wasn't enough. He'd left his jacket up at the winery when
he'd gone there in the afternoon to help unload one of the
gondolas. The fog had burned off, the sun was hot, he'd
taken his jacket off and hung it just inside a door to the
building the gringos called the "cuvier" where they pumped
the crushed grapes into big steel fermentation vats.

He knew the winery was strictly off-limits to the pickers
after work hours. But that night two years ago, he'd gone
anyway, slipping quietly through the dark. The door was
open and when he'd stepped inside he'd seen first the light,
then the man up on the huge two-thousand gallon vat pour-
ing something into it from a can. In the reflected beam of a
flashlight, he'd seen the man's face clearly.

He'd turned to leave and the man had heard him, had
swung the light around, and had seen him. So he'd run like
the devil back out of the building to his dormitory without
ever getting his jacket.

The next day the boss had pulled them all off the job.
Something about poison being put into one of the vats so
that the whole harvest was ruined and there was no point
in picking grapes anymore. They'd been trucked to another

vineyard across the valley, a much bigger one, and he'd picked there for ten days and then gone back to Mexico to his wife and three children.

Then today, at the same small vineyard in the hills, he'd seen the same gringo staring at him, not once but several times, not ordering him about as usual but just staring silently, and there was something in his eyes that told Julio not to stay there a minute longer. Something that made a cold tunnel of fear speard through his whole innards.

Now, with his head down and shoulders hunched, he was almost aware of the headlights behind him, a white glare diffused by the fog, until the car was nearly on him. But he did see, finally, and stepped quickly into the ditch beside the road.

The car slowed, passed, and stopped. He was at once uneasy. No gringo ever gave a ride to a Mexican worker. Then the car reversed, passed him again, and stopped a few yards back up the road. He heard one of the doors open, heard voices from inside the car, and a man appeared, silhouetted by the headlights. Julio couldn't see who it was, the lights half-blinded him, but he could see the shotgun cradled over the man's arm, and the tunnel of fear he'd felt in his innards came back and became everything in him. He wanted to run off into the fog. But he couldn't move. It had to be the man he'd seen and he'd waited too long to leave.

"Come here."

Yes, it was him, he recognized the voice. He stepped back into the road.

"Turn around."

When he didn't move, the gun barrel slapped hard across his face and he obeyed.

"Kneel down."

"Señor, I see nothing. I not hurt you. I go home now to Mexico."

And the gun barrel jabbed hard into his backbone. A scream of pain ran up to his head.

"Kneel."

He obeyed again. Slowly. He was going to die, he knew it now. The gun would blow half his head off. He thought of his wife and children and his home in the village outside Guadalajara. They would be around the table in one room they all lived in, eating dinner. Maybe they would never know what had happened to him. His wife would think he'd stayed in Los Estados Unidos. She would think there was another woman and she would cry and his children, too. And have to go into the streets for food or scavenge the city dump.

The surface of the road felt hard and wet. He took off his hat and held it against his thin chest and began to pray. "Jesu . . ."

He got no further. The butt of the shotgun smashed into the back of his head and he fell forward, his hat still clenched under him in his hands.

The man with the gun got back into the car and then carefully and deliberately drove it over Julio's inert body; once over the body, then, backing up, over his head, crushing his skull like a melon. The man got out to make sure Julio would never speak again, carefully avoiding the blood that poured out onto the road. Satisfied, he got back behind the wheel and drove over Julio again and off into the darkness.

Nobody found the Mexican until early morning, and there were crows there already, feeding.

THE "HIT-AND-RUN" DEATH of a poor Mexican grape picker in California's Napa Valley, which went unreported except for a few cryptic lines in a local newpaper, was something I could hardly have been aware of, even though I was in California at the time and only a few miles away. And if for some reason I had learned of it, it would have meant nothing to me anyway.

Two nights later I was a guest at a large cocktail party given by the wealthy owner of a sumptuous home in the low hills outside the old Victorian town of Napa itself, at the valley's southern end. The occasion was to mark the end of an annual rally of the region's hot-air balloon club which I'd come out from New York ten days earlier to participate in. There were a lot of people, a pianist was playing nostalgic oldies, and I was having a good time. After a week of being grubby and unfeminine in a nylon flight suit and combat boots, I'd gratefully washed and blow-dried my hair, put on a pretty strapless linen dress I'd bought in Italy, adorned myself with my favorite perfume, my pearl necklace, and my diamond-and-pearl earrings, and had been careful with my makeup.

Feeling an entirely new woman, I was on my first glass of champagne when I found myself confronted by a man in his mid-forties who was especially good-looking in a rugged outdoor way and who had unabashed deviltry in his eyes. He told me his name, which I didn't catch in the swirl of conversational noise around us—although he got mine, Margaret Barlow—and then launched into what I immediately suspected was a well-proven line of such outrageous flattery that I soon found myself laughing at everything he said.

Admittedly, I'm not doing badly for my age, which I stopped telling when I hit fifty. I have only the minimum of silver streaks amid the blond. Ditto, telltale lines in my face. And with the help of daily running and quite a bit of weekend tennis, my figure is still pretty much what it was when I was thirty. I hardly merited, however, being asked if I wasn't a famous fashion model. Or if he hadn't seen me on television.

"Look," I said finally. "Slow down. I'm the one supposed to be asking questions."

"Oh?"

"Oh, indeed!" I extracted my press card from my purse. Issued by the American League of Journalists, it contains only the barest essentials: my name, my occupation as a photo-journalist, a perfectly dreadful mug shot, and an "indefinite" expiration date. For some reason, it almost always stops people in their tracks, allowing me time to decide if I want to reveal anything more detailed about myself; for example, that I live in Manhattan in an apartment with a great view and summer with my two young grandchildren in an old house on Martha's Vineyard, that magical island off Cape Cod. Or that I'm a widow of some years after a long happy marriage to a great guy.

And it gives me a chance, too, to start with questions of my own.

"Now," I said firmly, when with a slightly suspicious look he handed me back my card. "Your name again, please. And your occupation. Where you got the terrific suntan and where you live."

I should have realized his recovery factor would be high. First he acted mock-surprised that I wouldn't know all those things about him. Then he said blandly, too blandly, "I'm a salesman."

I studied him, He smiled charmingly, waiting. And warning bells told me I was being set up. This one was more likely a Himalayan mountain climber or a round-the-world yachtsman.

But I played along. "Okay," I said. "Selling what?"

He looked around furtively and lowered his voice to a whisper. "Wine."

"And that's something in the Napa Valley you need to be mysterious about?"

He nodded. "This party's all sky people. I'm an undergrounder."

"Ah!" I said. "Of course. Wine cellars. Hence the suntan. Just one more question, then," I added. "Tell me. Exactly who or what winds you up every morning?"

He laughed and gave it up. "Touché," he said. "But that's something you get only over dinner." He glanced at his watch. "Say eight o'clock? San Francisco? That will give us time to consume more of our host's champagne first."

And I tried to keep the regret from my voice. "Sorry," I said. "No dinner. I have to work."

He looked genuinely taken aback. "Work?"

"A wine story. How it's made and marketed. Photos and text." Besides my press card I always carry a miniature camera just in case. Before he could speak again, I whipped it out of my purse and clicked off a close-up shot of his surprised expression. "You'll do for the picture of the salesman."

He didn't have the chance to protest. The balloon club president, a vast grizzled man in his seventies, with a girth like a balloon itself, loomed massively. He was the sort who booms rather than speaks. "Ah, there you are, young lady. I want you to meet an old friend." A good-natured roar and thump on the back of my would-be dinner date whom he clearly knew well—"You've terrorized her long enough!"— and I was literally bustled off before I could say another word.

I confess I wasn't too happy about that. I hadn't yet found out who my flirtatious stranger was. And I didn't see him again, except at a distance, and then conquering someone else twenty years my junior which left me feeling a little let down.

I didn't remain much longer at the party either. I couldn't. I did indeed have to go to work. A magazine had asked for a story on a quality Napa Valley winery and had arranged for me to visit the Abbaye de Ste. Denise, in the northern part of the valley, when the balloon rally was over. The owner, John Seldridge, was married to the film star Elissa Michaels, who had abandoned Hollywood some five years previous in favor of his vineyards, and had already become a well-known figure in the wine business. I had called her when I first arrived in California and she'd insisted I stay with them as long as I wished while I photographed and researched. "We'll just be beginning to harvest so you'll really be able to understand wine and how it's made," she said. "We'll expect you for dinner Friday night."

I was delighted, of course. My publisher had told me that the Abbaye was founded two hundred years ago by French Jesuits expelled from Mexico by the Spanish and was one of the loveliest places in America. Getting to know Elissa Michaels would also be interesting. I might even come away with more than just an article on wine.

The thirty-five-mile-long Napa Valley, which runs almost true north to south and is named after the river Napa that flows down through the middle, begins only some ten miles from the swampy northernmost extremes of San Francisco Bay. The town of St. Helena was seventeen miles futher up it from where I was and the Abbaye de Ste. Denise just beyond in the Mayacama Mountains which form the valley's western flank, separating it from the neighboring country and valley of Sonoma.

I'd looked down on all of it from the air late in the morning just the day before, drifting through clear hot sunny skies at six thousand feet and seeing through the rapidly dissipating blanket of white fog which nightly poured up the valley's length to be burned off by the sun before noon, its wide flat floor filled with vineyards; the grapevines pale green against the brown of the earth. In the Mayacamas and in the partially arid hills across the valley to the east, more vineyards nestled here and there in stark contrast to the darker green forests of pine and oak.

Except for its visual beauty, none of it meant much to me at the time. I had yet to know of the lengthy and complex process between picking grapes on a vine and pulling the cork on a vintage bottle of, say, Cabernet Sauvignon.

It was close to seven in the evening when I left Napa in a rental car. I took Highway 29 north up the middle of the valley, surprised by the commerciality which assaulted me from all sides. From the air you don't see the endless billboards, fast-food places, and drive-in souvenir shops. I'd expected a peaceful agricultural rurality that clearly no longer existed, and I had the immediate impression that promoting the wines of the Napa Valley had become almost a more important business than the wines themselves. When, just beyond the town of Yountville, the road narrowed, I began to see more and more signs for some of the valley's scores of vineyards and wineries. Markham, Mondavi, Stag's Leap Wine Cellars, Beringer, and Trefethen were names vaguely familiar to me.

Some five miles north of the town of St. Helena, a sign, smaller and rather more conservative than most, pointed off to my left and read: "L'Abbaye de Ste. Denise—John Seldridge, Vintner." Following Elissa's instructions, I turned into a narrow macadam country road which went past a large vineyard bordered by a windbreak of Lombardy poplars with an occasional giant palm.

Then, the road abruptly left the valley and snaked up a narrow canyon filled with redwood, eucalyptus, oak, and walnut trees, keeping just above a small stream until it suddenly burst out onto a wide saddle between two rounded hills.

The sun was very low and I was shading my eyes from it when I first glimpsed, close by the road, a cluster of buildings whose upper floors and tiled roofs were visible over a high stone wall on my right, broken by two huge forged-iron gates. As I got nearer, I saw a sign similar to the one in the valley. I had arrived at L'Abbaye de Ste. Denise.

2

THE GATES WERE SHUT and there seemed to be nobody around, but I saw a brass push-button bell set in the stone next to them. I got out of my car, pressed it, and waited for something to happen. While I did, I peered through the gates and got my first good look at the Abbaye.

My publisher was right. I have known many lovely places in my life, but almost none could compare in beauty with the romantically pastoral setting I now saw.

Immediately to my left, the cluster of buildings that I'd seen, four in all, was identified by a small sign as the winery. Directly in front of me, a long gravel drive went by them and wound across a soft expanse of green lawn, broken here and there by the occasional giant eucalyptus or magnificent olive tree whose gnarled trunk spoke of great age, a grove or two of flowering oleander and hibiscus, and a large colorful flower bed set against a hedge of verdant box. At the end of the drive, and set against a hillside of vineyards that sloped gently up to the hill's spruce-covered crown, there was a very old and lovely two-story house of heavy cut-stone blocks once covered with adobe, now partially eroded away, and which over the years, like its tiled roof, had been bleached nearly white by the California sun. Here and there, climbing vines of morning glory, trumpet, and wisteria wove between the windows. I could see several cars parked in front of wide steps and a big, weathered oaken front door.

Halfway between it and the winery was another smaller and isolated building, a respectable distance from the drive and at the very edge of a vineyard. Partially hidden by a grove of oak trees and as old and weathered as the house, it was clearly once a barn or stable and now, from the several trucks and tractors parked there, seemed to be a utility building and garage.

I turned to look at the winery itself. The four buildings, also with sunbleached tiled roofs and adobe-plastered walls of hewn stone partially covered by climbing vines, formed a square around a sizable paved courtyard, or cloister. I could see much of this cloister through a wide archway in the building closest to me and the driveway. A small sculpted fountain in its worn, paved center, along with the slender stone columns of a loggia gracing one side of it, made me think of the monks who once must have filed silently past at this same hour on their way to vespers in the Abbaye's chapel. This was the building which, dominating the others, lay farthest away from me across the cloister and whose entrance was on the road running past the property.

As I stood there, taking it all in, there was a sudden clicking sound and the huge gates swung open slowly. It wasn't until I started to get back into my car that I noticed the closed-circuit TV camera pointing down at me from the wall and then the razor wire which topped the wall itself as well as the gates. Wondering at such security, I drove through and in the rearview mirror watched the gates close behind me, something which made me feel vaguely uncomfortable.

Continuing on to the house, I parked near a station wagon, a muddy and rather battered jeep, and a sleek, decidedly unbattered silver gray Ferrari. I had hardly retrieved my suitcase and a duffle bag filled with my cameras and flight gear from the trunk when the front door opened and a slender dark-haired woman in her early thirties appeared. She had on tight corduroy riding pants, jodhpur boots, and a colorful cotton shirt. I had no difficulty recognizing her. It was Elissa Michaels.

"Margaret Barlow?" Before I could answer, she decided I was and with a warm smile of greeting, came out to meet me.

"Hello, Margaret. I'm Elissa. I'm so sorry you found the gates closed. I asked John to leave them open for you and obviously he forgot. Come on in. May I help?" And before I could stop her, she hefted my heavy duffle bag with a strength that surprised me and led the way into the house.

Inside, I had two immediate impressions—age and coolness. It was as though the house was peopled not only by the Seldridges but by all the many abbots and bishops who had once resided there. The front hall was extremely large, going right up to the roof with two stairs, one beginning on the right side of the hall, the other on the left, sweeping up to join at the second-floor balcony.

The furnishings were all lovely old antiques. There was a long refectory table against one wall — eighteenth-century Spanish, I guessed, and wondered if it had been brought from Mexico by the Jesuits. It was graced by two tall iron candlesticks which I suspected had been lifted from the chapel altar and was flanked by two big brocaded Georgian armchairs. On the wall above, there was a large and beautiful old tapestry depicting a French grape harvest in medieval times. On the opposite side of the hall, across a flagstone floor only partially covered by two oriental rugs, was a high-backed seventeenth-century oak settle or bench. Next to it was the door, now open, to a small library and on the wall above, a collection of tools, mostly wooden, once used in the vineyards.

Elissa pointed to the stairs. "You're up there on the right, the Blue Room," she said briskly. "It's at the end of the corridor across from John and me and next to Lureen, John's stepdaughter. Did you want to go up now? We're outside on the terrace, John and his brother, Bryant. Dinner won't be for another thirty minutes. I hope you're not starving.''

I said I wasn't, declined upstairs for the moment, put my valise down next to where she'd set my duffle, and followed her through a short passageway under the balcony where there was a telephone alcove, then through open double-doors into the living room. Clearly the main family room, with deep couches, bookcases, piano, and television, it was cheerfully decorated in a country-style chintz.

French doors led from it onto a wide flagstone terrace just beyond which I saw a swimming pool. As we came out, two men rose politely to greet me. One was John Seldridge, the vintner and Elissa's husband, the other his brother, Bryant, a San Francisco lawyer. In their early forties, both were strong, well-built men, John especially so. Yet they hardly seemed brothers. John, the older, I guessed, by two or three years, had a mane of black hair and a darkly brooding, even surly quality about him which made you expect at any second that he'd make things difficult. Bryant, lighter haired and beginning to bald, wore glasses, had a totally infectious laugh, and was, on the other hand, one of those open friendly people who immediately put you at your ease. I was surprised to learn he was a bachelor. Both were dressed casually in jeans, with John wearing an old suede jacket over a T-shirt and Bryant a rather shabby sweater. John had on tattered sneakers and Bryant Topsiders. I felt decidedly overdressed in my strapless dress and jewelry even though I'd covered my bare shoulders with a cardigan against the coolness of the evening and had abandoned my heels, while driving, for an old pair of espadrilles.

I had the impression, even as I was being introduced, that I had interrupted some sort of a dispute. John, whose voice I had heard raised angrily as Elissa and I crossed the living room, became rather quiet after he went through the ritual of welcoming me. And I felt Bryant, in spite of his open friendliness, was covering nervousness about something.

Elissa took charge immediately. She saw that I was comfortably seated, ordered Bryant to fetch me a glass of cold white wine from a bottle in a nearby cooler, and at once began to ask me the questions a good hostess always asks of a guest, especially a stranger. How was my drive up from Napa? Was it my first visit to California? And I simply must tell them, she said, about ballooning. It sounded terribly exciting.

All the time I was keenly aware of the film star in her. She wasn't an especially beautiful woman, although she did have commanding good looks. But she had an almost magnetic quality about her along with an air of authoritative self-confidence that came from the security of fame and money. She also had the kind of warmth many actresses automatically project and which is often not necessarily real, and I found myself wondering how much of her manner was a front for another Elissa who might lie hidden somewhere. She was not, I felt, a woman I could get to know all that easily.

When I'd managed all the appropriate answers, I admired a lovely view of the vineyards rising up the hill and which began right beyond the swimming pool and now, with the sun set, were slowly fading into the purple of onrushing twilight. Their father, Simon Seldridge, had bought the place as a young man, Bryant told me. Newly married, he'd come to California from Chicago, after a honeymoon trip in the Bordeaux region of France, with a dream of making wine. Driving through the Napa Valley, he had turned off the highway and come up the canyon to fall upon the Abbaye in much the same manner as I had.

"That was fifty years ago," Bryant explained. "It was virtually a ruin, and he started making wine on only about five acres with equipment nobody today would even think of. There were only a handful of wineries in the valley then."

"Simon didn't care about quantity," Elissa said. "His only thought was to produce an estate wine equal to the very best the French could make. 'Estate' means wine made almost entirely from your own grapes. In France their term is *château.*" She put her hand possessively on John's. "And that is just what we are continuing to do."

"John and Elissa turn out the finest estate Cabernet Sauvignon in America," Bryant added. "Perhaps even in the world."

"How about yourself?" I asked.

He grinned cheerfully. "Me? They're the wine experts. The only thing I have to do with wine, outside of a little legal work for the Abbaye, is to come up here weekends from San Francisco and drink it."

"Don't you believe him," Elissa said to me. "He handles most of our business affairs, and brilliantly."

I didn't learn more at that moment. First, José, their Hispanic chef-butler, appeared to announce dinner would be in ten minutes. And then Lureen, John's stepdaughter, made her appearance.

Expecting an ordinarily pretty young woman, I was taken by surprise. She was twenty, I guessed, and with her dark smoldering eyes, full sensual mouth, and sculpted cheekbones, she was a natural beauty to put many to shame. And she had taken steps to make herself even more striking. She'd cut her dark brunette hair short like a man's and wore no makeup or jewelry except large gold hoop earrings. But she had muted this masculine appearance with a skin-tight body suit which unabashedly showed the near perfection of her superbly muscular yet stunningly feminine body to the fullest advantage, leaving almost nothing to the imagination. I couldn't help but wonder why she'd dress such a way for a quiet family evening at home.

We were introduced, and she greeted me politely in an attractively low and husky voice which somehow perfectly matched her appearance. But I got the feeling that the greeting was merely perfunctory; that she would have little curiosity about anyone outside her own immediate clique of beautiful people.

With her arrival, an additional undercurrent of tension immediately entered the atmosphere. John, Elissa, and even

Bryant all suddenly seemed to choose their words carefully. I was relieved when we went into dinner.

In the candlelit dining room whose furnishings were as old and elegant as those in the hall, I met the patriarch from whom all this had begun. Although only a portrait, Simon Seldridge seemed to dominate the room. There was no escaping his severe gray eyes. Strangely, his portraitist had chosen to paint him not against a background of vineyards or even perhaps oak wine barrels, but in hunting garb, rifle in one hand, rough-rider hat in the other, standing over the body of a mountain lion. He was a handsome old bull, no question of that, with strength, purposefulness, and an iron will written into every feature. I didn't care at all for the picture, though. I thought the background in bad taste and the all-seeing eyes most disturbing, even embarrassing, as if his two sons were still schoolboys who needed supervision. I found myself thinking I wouldn't have wanted to be either of them when young.

Dinner was excellent and included the best wine I've ever tasted, which Bryant proudly told me was their 1983 reserve Cabernet Sauvignon. But my pleasure was somewhat dimmed by what I thought was slightly forced small talk that he and Elissa maintained throughout the meal, while Lureen and John, although polite, hardly spoke at all.

Where John was concerned, I soon began to suspect I'd be faced with a real challenge getting the information about vineyards and wineries that I was going to need. My publisher had said, "Seldridge was raised on wine; he's forgotten more about it than most American vintners will ever know." But as dinner wore on, John didn't seem to care at all about a magazine article featuring his vineyard. He displayed a haughty, almost Olympian remoteness which reflected, I thought, the bored snobbishness of the artist and intellectual toward the layman. He would talk volubly with other wine experts and connoisseurs, I was certain, but when it came to someone like me and to practicalities, it was obvious he didn't really want to make an effort. I found it difficult to discover anything in him I liked—there was enough ego there, I thought, for three people—and wondered what Elissa saw in him.

I was beginning to feel frustrated and slightly discouraged with my whole visit when, quite unexpectedly, something happened that obviously wasn't supposed to. It came from Lureen. As we rose to go to the living room for coffee, she suddenly said to me, "When will your article appear, Mrs. Barlow?"

And when I told her not for at least six months, she said "Well, if it's that long a time it could be a waste of your effort. Perhaps Elissa forgot to mention it, but the chances are pretty good we won't be in business anymore by then."

In the dead silence that followed, she smiled challengingly at Elissa who, for an instant, looked furious but then recovered quickly and with a laugh, albeit one I thought theatrical, said to me, "It's been a long haul to get the Abbaye to where it is today. Old Simon left it in quite a mess, actually, and Lureen's always been doubtful we'd ever make it. I can't blame her. Sometimes I didn't think we would myself. But we have."

Unfazed, Lureen locked eyes with her. "Elissa, you mean you hope we have. But if we get sabotaged again this year, we'll have to shut down, won't we?"

Elissa had by then gained complete control of herself. She favored Lureen with an indulgent smile. "Darling, we all promised to put that unfortunate business behind us and never to think or speak of it again, didn't we?" And then, as though Lureen had never spoken, she turned quickly to Bryant, "Bryant, did you remember to bring the insurance forms Lureen has to fill out?"

He picked up on it at once. "Of course. I have them right here." He pulled an envelope from a pocket.

"Good. Then perhaps before Lureen turns in?"

"Sure. We can do it right now. Lureen?"

He took Lureen's elbow. She laughed and, without resisting, went with him across the hall to the library. As they reached the door, she looked back and called out, "Good night, Mrs. Barlow." It was clearly directed at Elissa and in a tone that was defiantly mocking. My immediate thought was that in this family there had to be many a head-on collision between stepmother and stepdaughter.

Elissa carried it off beautifully. She acted as though she hadn't heard, and she and John and I went on to the living room. John, however, was obviously annoyed by the exchange, and I was immediately intrigued, knowing I had stumbled onto something being deliberately kept from me.

I decided, however, not to ask any questions for the moment. The truth would surface soon enough with a minimum of effort on my part, I thought, if I were patient. No further mention of the incident was made while we had coffee in the living room, but as I surmised I was not to be kept in the dark very long.

LUREEN WENT UP TO BED directly after she and Bryant had
dealt with the insurance forms. Bryant joined Elissa, John,
and me to lighten the evening with amusing stories about
winemakers and his flourishing law practice. Then, when
we all called it a night, he went off to the room he always
used on weekends at the Abbaye and I went with Elissa up
to mine.

The Blue Room was down a wide hall and separated from
Lureen's room by a bathroom, with both rooms being directly across from Elissa and John's and another guest room
and bath. A small back stair at the very end of the hall went
down to the kitchen, Elissa told me, and just as we were
entering the Blue Room, Lureen, in a smart cotton nightshirt,
appeared at the top of it with a can of Coke and some cookies.
She favored us with a fleeting half-smile and a murmured
"Good night" as she went by but rather to my relief didn't
speak further, and I heard the door to her room close firmly
behind her.

The Blue Room was lovely, with an old French provincial
armoire and a big four-poster bed, its bedspread and curtains

of a delicate blue floral pattern to match similar wallpaper and pale blue bathroom fixtures.

Elissa had showed me where everything was kept and was preparing to leave when I decided to try cautiously to see if this wouldn't be the right moment to satisfy my curiosity.

"It's been a wonderful evening," I said, deliberately hesitating before adding "but I can't help feeling I might have interrupted something private. I'm so sorry if I have."

Elissa studied me, then smiled and said lightly, "You're very observant, Margaret, but please don't worry yourself. You just happened to have come in on a minor family dispute. Nothing important. I do hope we haven't made you feel uncomfortable."

"Not at all, every family has its problems."

"Yes," she said. Nothing more. And then she abruptly said good night and started for the door.

I mentally kicked myself, certain I'd acted too precipitously. I was wrong. Quite suddenly she stopped and turned around and her whole manner was different. She was no longer Elissa Michaels, the film star, but Elissa Seldridge, the winemaker, and strictly business.

"Okay," she said. "It wasn't just a minor family dispute and I think it might be better if I cleared the air and told you all about it, regardless of the risk to your article with all its publicity value to us. If I don't and after what Lureen said tonight, you're either going to hear more from her or be curious enough to find out on your own and you might not get a straight story."

I sat down on the edge of the bed. "Sure," I said. "Go ahead."

She took an upholstered chair facing me. "First, we probably owe you an apology for ever agreeing to your using the Abbaye as a background for your wine story because Lureen is right. We're in trouble and could possibly have to shut down. We very selfishly, I suppose, just saw a great publicity break."

I thought of her husband's surprisingly aloof indifference at dinner and said nothing.

"And it does have to do with sabotage," Elissa went on. "Two years ago someone poured a gallon of pesticide into one of our main fermentation vats and we lost our Cabernet Sauvignon harvest. And lost the Chardonnay grape and Pinot Noir harvests, too, which followed, because the health department closed us down until every vat, pipe, and pump in the place could be inspected. That took weeks and the grapes rotted on the vine before we could sell them to another winery.

"Then, last year, we lost the harvest again because somebody got into the utility building where we keep all our vineyard machinery. Gasoline was poured over our new mechanical grape picker and then a match tossed in. The only reason the whole building didn't go up was that our viticulturist, Roland Grunnigen, has an apartment there. He got extinguishers and a hose going but it was too late for the picker. And it was too late to round up migrant Mexican workers which is how we always used to harvest."

"Are you using them this year again?"

"Yes, but wait." Elissa held up her hand. "There's more. Last spring we started getting anonymous letters saying we'd be hit again this year. We turned them over to the police but so far they haven't been able to trace them. That's why all the security out front, the TV cameras and the razor wire, in addition to our regular alarm system, which almost everyone in the valley uses to protect their cellars from theft.

"And then," she continued, "two days ago there was the Mexican. I can't remember his name." She shrugged. "Garcia something. Apparently he picked for us two years ago when we were ruined by the pesticide and came again this year. The police found him after the first day of work on the road down in the valley. They first concluded that he was a hit-and-run victim, but later the medical examiner discovered he had received a blow to his head *before* he was run over. So it was murder. And not by another Mexican worker;

none of them have cars. The police think he might have been killed because he knew whoever it was who sabotaged us two years ago. Anyway, that's what Lureen meant. I've sunk all my film earnings into this place, John's put in every penny he had, and Bryant quite a bit, too. We're existing on bank loans and the banks threaten to foreclose on us every day because they know we're living on our previous years' vintages and that two years down the line our earnings will dry up. We sleep nights with our fingers crossed."

I quickly added it up. Clearly the Seldridges were a family living virtually in a state of siege. "Who has it in for you?" I asked. "And why."

"The who is up for grabs," she answered. "But the why seems pretty clear. Somebody wants to ruin us so they can get the Abbaye. They figure we'll be forced to sell to avoid going bankrupt, and this place is worth a fortune. You see, in addition to the winery and the vineyards right around here, we have a hundred and fifty more acres of hilltop we don't cultivate because at the moment we can't afford to."

"Then wouldn't it make sense to sell just them?" I asked.

"We can't," Elissa told me. "We're not allowed to. A condition of old Simon's will is that the whole place has to be kept together."

I thought of the all-seeing eyes of the portrait in the dining room and the power of the man after death. It seemed unfair, but perhaps in a way he was right. If part of a property was sold every time there was trouble, one could end up with nothing.

I asked if the police had any leads at all in finding the saboteur.

Elissa shook her head. "None. It could be anyone, an outsider who wants into the wine business. Another estate winery like us who wants to grow more of its own and can't find land at a price it can afford. Or a plain ordinary grower like Harry Charwood down in the valley. He's constantly making us offers. Harry's not a winery; he sells his grapes to some giant like Turbo Wines in the Central Valley. They do forty million cases a year for supermarket jug sales and will take almost anything as long as it comes off a vine. A grower is the most likely suspect because they would probably sell the house and the winery to a hotel or some other institution to help recoup part of the overall purchase price." She laughed. "But nobody could ever suspect Harry. He's the original clown."

It seemed to me an impossible situation to live with. "Have you ever considered selling out completely and starting a new winery somewhere else?"

Elissa nodded. "Oh yes. Where the land is less expensive. We've talked about it. Bryant, I think, would like to. But John loves this place. He's put his whole life into it. If it can possibly be saved, he wants to."

"How do you feel?"

"In between," she admitted. "It depends on the banks on the day in question. Or how the other two shareholders feel."

I hadn't realized there were shareholders. "John's not the sole owner?"

She hesitated just an instant before answering, "No, Simon left it to both John and Bryant."

Who was the third person, then? And how could there be a third owner if the property was left to the two brothers? I didn't have a chance to ask. Elissa glanced at her watch. "Oh, Heavens," she said. "Look at the time. I've gone on much too long. And anyway, that's it. If we get through this year, we'll be out of the woods. We'll probably know within a week. Harvesting will be mostly over then. But if Lureen turns out to be right and we have more trouble, your article could end up dead news and not worth any more of your time. Now that you know, perhaps in the morning you could tell me whether you still want to go on with it."

I didn't hesitate long in answering. My story was on quality wine and how it was made. It would be for my editor to decide if the Abbaye's possibly going broke would make any difference to it.

"I can tell you right now," I said. "I can't see any reason not to."

She looked surprised, even slightly taken aback, but then put a warmly solicitous hand over mine. "Margaret, are you sure?"

The gesture suddenly made me feel that she was trying to put me off. But why? Before Lureen had let the cat out of the bag, sabotage and murder apparently hadn't made Elissa concerned about the time and work I'd put into my article, so I could hardly believe she was genuinely worried now. Was there something else that Lureen's indiscretion might now cause to surface that she didn't want me to know about?

Sitting at the end of the lovely old four-poster, I suddenly had an overwhelming curiosity to find out. "Quite sure," I said firmly. "As long as my being here doesn't inconvenience you too much."

If it was not what she wanted to hear, she showed no sign. Her smile was graciousness itself. "Of course not, Margaret. The place is yours. Make yourself at home, please. We'll give you all the help we can."

Then she rose abruptly and went to the door. Elissa Seldridge, the winemaker, had disappeared and Elissa Michaels, the film star, was back again, posed dazzlingly. Which was the real woman? Or was neither one? I still didn't know.

"What do you take for breakfast?"

I told her just coffee and toast and she said to sleep as long as I liked in the morning and good night and the next second was gone, the door closing softly behind her.

I was dog-tired, so tired I didn't even lock my door which I usually always do when in a strange house. I went gratefully to bed but for a while was unable to sleep. I had a gut feeling that the dirty tricks Elissa told me about might well get dirtier and that I could get a lot more for my pains than a straightforward photo story on wine.

The feeling made me shiver with expectation. I'd had it before one terrible summer in Martha's Vineyard when I'd found myself for the first time ever confronted by murder. And then again when murder stalked Brides Hall prep school, my old alma mater on Maryland's Eastern Shore. No matter what the circumstances, depriving another of life can never be condoned and both times I'd been compelled by a determination to expose whomever was guilty and not leave it to chance that the law would eventually catch up with them. Now, here was murder once more. Even though I didn't know him, I'd felt anger on hearing of the poor Mexican worker and the terribly cruel way he'd died, the same sort of deep anger I'd felt over those other murders. Anger and sadness, too, for I didn't think many in the Napa Valley, so far from his home, cared very much what had happened to him and why.

But I did, and I fell asleep, finally, wondering if he had a family and who would look after them now that he was gone. And with my mind made up that one day they would know who had taken him from them.

I WAS AWAKENED in the morning by the distinctive sound of a tractor. Rising to look out the window, I saw it, driven by a muscular young man who sat high above the vines, coming out from the vineyard through the last remaining swirls of Napa Valley nighttime fog and onto a narrow track just beyond the swimming pool. A long narrow gondola loaded with fresh-picked grapes was being pulled behind. I heard shouts in Spanish and then made out a score of men halfway up the hill cutting grapes away from the vines.

I looked at my leather-cased travel clock on the bedside table. It was nearly nine. Feeling guilty at having slept so late, I showered, put on a skirt and blouse and sandals, threw a cardigan over my shoulders, and went downstairs to coffee and toast on the terrace.

There was nobody around. José, the butler, told me Elissa had gone into St. Helena and that John was up at the winery. "And Mr. Bryant is up there, too, Mrs. Barlow. In the office."

I didn't ask about Lureen. I just presumed, given her age and lack of occupation as well as what seemed to be her character, that she'd still be asleep.

I had finished a second cup of coffee when I heard the

French doors behind me open and presumed it was José until the relative silence of the terrace was abruptly broken by a cold feminine voice demanding, "Who are you, please?"

Startled, I turned. The woman who addressed me was about as chilling a number as I would ever want to meet. A tall, overly lacquered platinum blonde in her forties, she had almost perfect features painted heavily with makeup and clearly half-sculpted by cosmetic surgery. Her eyes were like ice. Her clothes were recognizably designer labels and she wore enough jewelry for three women. Here was money, I thought, but very little class or taste.

I identified myself and waited for her to do the same. She didn't. Instead, she simply stared at me silently, the arrogance in her expression matching her previous tone of voice. José saved the day. He appeared from the living room and said, "Good morning Miss Hester."

She didn't return José's courtesy either. She said only, "Where's Lureen?"

"I haven't seen her yet this morning, madam."

Her reply was to go back inside the house without a word.

"Lureen's mother?" I asked.

José nodded.

I heard her twice loudly call out, "Lureen?" Then silence.

José cleared my breakfast coffee with no comment but then as he started to leave the terrace, said, sotto voce, "She's taking Miss Lureen shopping today and we'll have her for dinner, too, most likely."

For dinner? The ex-wife? My disbelief grew.

I went into the house and then, crossing the front hall to go upstairs, ran into both mother and daughter on their way out. I said good morning to Lureen and she returned the greeting. But Hester Seldridge walked past me as though I didn't exist. Outside, they got into a smart new Mercedes convertible and drove away.

I was still standing there, coping with my surprise and my

burgeoning resentment at the rudeness, when a voice right behind me made me start.

"I see you've met our Hester."

I turned. It was Bryant, wearing a big grin, his eyes laughing behind his glasses. I admitted I had and didn't have to say more. I got an immediate explanation as to why she was able to walk about the Abbaye as though she owned it.

"Everyone has a cross to bear, I suppose," he said, his smile fading, "and she's ours. She owns a share of this place. John and I would give almost anything to get rid of her."

So that was it. The third shareholder. And that, I imagined, for Elissa, too, had to be worse than a cross.

"Now," Bryant said, brightening again, "it's tour time. Unlike the large groups at all the other wineries in the Napa Valley, you get your own personal guide."

He gave me five minutes to change into running shoes and jeans. I did and, loaded with all my camera gear, found myself embarked on a tour more strenuous than I could ever have imagined, during which I learned that between the appearance of a first tender spring shoot on a vine and the lovely deep red or the palest primrose white in a glass of wine several years later, there is a long and intricate process.

I was to learn how the mineral content and drainage of the soil affected the taste of the ultimate wine as well as vineyard temperature and how much sun and rain the growing grapes received. And that each of the scores of different kinds of grapes in the world, once harvested and crushed, needed different fermentation temperatures, usually for several weeks in sterile stainless-steel tanks, afterward aging in oak barrels for three or four years with the kind of oak, chosen from different parts of the world, equally important to the wine's taste.

We started in the part of the vineyards devoted to the Merlot grape, one of the "greats," Bryant explained. "It matures earlier than the others. So we pick it first. And it's critically important to us. Our principal product is a Bordeaux red, and Bordeaux is traditionally a mixture of several grapes with Cabernet Sauvignon the dominant one. Cabernet gives the wine its basic body and strength. The Merlot is added to give it a softness."

We walked the vineyards until my legs felt like lead. It was very warm and while part of me yearned to be back up in a balloon in the cool air of five thousand feet, part of me tried to absorb facts like tons of grapes produced per acre; a calculation into something called "hectoliters"; whether to irrigate or to sprinkle the vines; which ones were most susceptible to which diseases and grubs; the importance of fog to Napa Valley production—it keeps the ripening grapes from overheating—and a million other complexities I soon forgot.

Watching the Mexican pickers, I again thought of the one Elissa said had been murdered, and felt sure that wine-making was somehow probably behind his death. It seemed forever before we left the vineyards for the winery itself. We followed a tractor pulling a big gondola loaded with Merlot grapes through the archway entrance to the stone-paved cloister and to a wide doorway in the once monastic dormitory bordering on the road. There, an electric motor tightened a cable from a gantry attached to one side of the gondola, tipping it over, so that its contents spilled into the funnel mouth of a big steel hopper, the rim of which was flush with the building's floor.

Looking down over a security rail, I saw the grapes tumbling, leaves, stalks and all, down onto a big Archimedian screw at the bottom of the hooper, which, turning around and around, pulled them through a tight aperture and out of sight.

"That's the crusher-stemmer," Bryant explained. "It gets rid of the leaves and stalks and crushes the grapes, skins and all, into juice, which is pumped into a vat to ferment."

I kept thinking of all the pictures I'd ever seen of bare-legged, bare-footed, and sometimes completely naked peasant men and women tramping about in great open wooden tubs crushing grapes with their feet.

John was there, getting a reading from a small instrument. "Checking the sugar/acid balance," Bryant told me. We all spoke a moment. John was brusque, barely taking time to give me the most impatient of greetings before he returned to his work. I managed not to look too taken aback and commented only on how harried he seemed. Bryant laughed. "Don't mind John. He always gets this way at harvest time," he said. "He only has to make one small error in judgment and we've got a bad year in bottles."

I watched a workman dumping small amounts of what I was told was sulphur dioxide into the hopper to kill unwanted bacteria and keep the wine from turning brown, and then Bryant took me into the building itself where after all the heat of the vineyard, the coolness was sheer heaven and where save for the faint rumbling of the crusher-stemmer beneath us in the cellar, the silence was intense.

The entire second floor had been removed so that there was a clear space right to the roof from the ground. This was called the "cuvier," I was told, and it was filled with shining stainless-steel vats, some holding twenty thousand gallons, others no more than five hundred. Around the walls, a network of shining pipes brought the juice of pressed grapes to the tanks and took it away again once turned into wine by fermentation.

I reloaded my camera with film, then we went down into the faintly lit cellars built so long ago by the loving hands of migrant French monks. There, the ancient stone of the vaulted ceilings, the even cooler temperature, the dark shadows, the row upon row of oak barrels large and small, the seemingly endless neatly stacked bottles, the heady smell of wine—all this to me finally *was* wine. I paid little attention to Bryant while he talked about yearly "racking," the emptying of each barrel into another; or about the "bouquet" and "elegance" and "finish" of the wine he drew from one oak cask to be tasted; nor his muttering an apology about a bottle he opened for it's being "musty," "dumb," and "un-resolved," probably, he said, because it had come from a cask where there was a rotten stave.

We sat on barrels in the vaulted gloom and chatted, and I just felt and saw and thought of cowled Jesuit monks, now the dust of centuries, tending wine in the same cellar by candlelight, and enjoyed Bryant's warm friendliness and the great wine we drank. The precious moment was my reward, I decided, for having staggered in slightly less than four hours through the four-year or more process which had got the wine into my glass.

And, as it turned out, it was also a momentary reprieve from as much horror as I care ever to encounter again.

I ASKED BRYANT why he hadn't followed in his father's footsteps like John and become a vintner. He seemed so knowledgeable.

"I suppose I am," he replied with a laugh, "because wine is all we ever heard in our house morning, noon, and night while we were growing up. Our mother died when John and I were very young, and our father couldn't imagine his two sons not having the same love for it that he did. He looked to us both to take over the winery when he was gone, and he made us work all our school vacations in the winery, or in the vineyards. He even sent us to France to learn how the French do it. John always loved it but in college I decided the law interested me more."

"Was your father desperately disappointed?"

"He was, but in time he got used to it and ended up having me do all his legal work. And since he left me a half share of the Abbaye, I still do and help out with the business end of things." He shook his head. "John's a great vintner, but he's hopeless when it comes down to hard practicalities."

"Elissa told me you'd probably just as soon sell out here and buy a less expensive place elsewhere."

"True," he said. "John and I argue about it occasionally. But in good times the Abbaye can pay a handsome return, and, more importantly, this place is John's universe, so I usually let him win."

"Was that the argument that was going on the night I arrived?" I asked.

"Not an argument, really. It's just that John gets awfully hot under the collar sometimes. I'd hinted we'd received an offer. Only hinted. He was tired, I guess. Harvest is tough on the nerves."

I still felt there was more, but instead asked about Hester.

"How did she ever end up a part-owner?" I asked. "Did that come about through her marriage to John?"

"And divorce," he answered. "When she and John were divorced, the court under California's property division law gave her half of his half-share."

"So he only has a quarter share now?"

"Correct."

"Were they married long?"

He shook his head. "Only a few years. If you want to call it a marriage. She was never home. She stayed with John just long enough for our father to die so she could hit John for a big inheritance—she thought. Well, she thought wrong." He laughed. "I'll never forget her face when I told her Simon died broke. He ran the winery badly the last few years of his life—he was far too busy playing the role of the granddaddy vintner of the Napa Valley—and it's taken poor old John ever since to try to put the place back on its feet. He'd almost succeeded, too, when the sabotaging began. Elissa told me she talked to you about it."

"Yes," I said. "It's awful."

Bryant's quietly humorous eyes darkened. "If I ever catch the son of a bitch who did it," he muttered, "God help him. And I'll give him extra for the poor Mexican. It had to be the same person."

"In the divorce, was John awarded Lureen's custody?" I asked.

"Yes. Hester didn't want her. She's not Lureen's real mother, you see. Lureen was adopted by Hester's first husband and his wife before Hester. The wife walked out on him and Lureen, he married Hester, and then he died. Hester was stuck with Lureen and when she and John divorced, she dumped her on him as fast as she could. He felt sorry for the child and did the best he could alone and then Elissa came along. I think the only reason Hester takes Lureen shopping is to irritate him. Beats me why she bothers. She never loved him or Lureen."

"A case of I don't want her but you can't have her?" I asked.

"I wouldn't argue with that," he agreed.

"What about Lureen?" I asked. "How does she feel about Hester?"

"I don't think there's much love lost there either."

"But, just the same, Lureen goes shopping with her."

Bryant shrugged. "What can you do? Lureen, bless her, travels with a fast crowd with expensive taste and money to match, when these days money for her is slow, if at all. Hester fills the gap. Lureen's always been the same way about men," he added. "If there's money there, fine. If not, forget it. Sometimes that's been pretty upsetting for John".

We walked on through the cellars and I asked Bryant why he'd never married.

"Maybe no one would have me."

"Liar."

He laughed and wanted to know about my marriage and my life since my husband died, and I was glad of his company. Although I welcomed the coolness and quiet of the cellars, I didn't think I'd particularly want to be in them by myself; after a while their dim gloom became a little oppressive. In one particularly badly lit area, we came onto a rusty iron gate behind which was a dark vaulted room, heaped with skulls and bones—the Jesuit monks' ossuary, fascinating but chilling, too.

"We could easily turn it into a major tourist attraction," Bryant said, "but John won't hear of it."

The labyrinth went under the cloister into the crypt of the chapel where we climbed a narrow stone stairway, deeply worn by the feet of countless monks over the years, and came into the chapel itself. I was at once struck by the simple beauty of the place; by the high arched rafters under the tiled roof where here and there a swallow swooped from its nest in silent flight; by the rows of scarred old oaken pews and the simple stone font; and finally by the hand-carved wooden Christ-crucified, its once gaudy hues faded to mute earth colors. The chapel was rarely ever used, Bryant explained, except for very special occasions, but Elissa saw that it was kept clean and tidy, and free of bats and other vermin.

We went through a small door into what I guessed was the vestry and from there up a little spiral stairway.

"The back way to the office," Bryant told me. "The main entrance is from the cloister itself, the loggia side."

At the top of the stairway, a short narrow passage led into the adjoining building. At the end of it, Bryant opened another door and the large reception room in which I suddenly found myself was a total contrast to the winery's antiquity. The indirect lighting and furniture were modern, the walls covered with beautiful photo murals of vineyard and winery activity. Off it, there were offices.

"One is mine, one John's," Bryant said. "And the third office Hester insists on keeping for herself although she never uses it."

We heard voices and I followed him into a large secretarial room which, since it was the weekend, was empty. Across it were two other executive offices and in one I met two people. First, there was Roland Grunnigen, the Abbaye's viticulturist, the man responsible for the vineyards themselves. With him was Alice Brooks, in charge of marketing and publicity.

I realized I'd already seen Grunnigen. He was the muscular

young man, far too self-consciously macho and aware of his own good looks for my liking, who had been on the tractor earlier that morning. He had a slight French accent, a thin, cruel mouth, and eyes that did not smile. I was sure he spent a lot of time in front of mirrors.

My reaction to Alice was different although I'm not certain whether I liked her or was simply touched by her. About forty and prematurely gray, she was the kind of woman who had always saddened me. Obviously once quite beautiful, and still good looking in a Junoesque way, her features had been eroded by life's disappointments and by drink, too, I suspected.

While Bryant made a phone call and then spoke to Grunnigen about a dispute which had arisen over the Mexican pickers' wages, Alice and I talked. She had been the liaison with my magazine publisher and we discussed the article. She filled me in, too, on a recent Abbaye triumph she'd engineered: the promotion by an important New York restaurant of the Abbaye's best Cabernet Sauvignon, a twelve-year-old vintage.

As she spoke, I had a strong feeling that she'd been crying before we came in; her eyes were far too glassy and bright, and I wondered if once more at the Abbaye I hadn't walked in on something private.

Bryant and I had a late lunch together. He then had office work to do, and I spent the afternoon taking more pictures and wondering what might unfold when Hester and Lureen returned from shopping. I didn't have to wonder long. They showed up, both loaded with shopping bags from expensive boutiques, as Elissa, John, Bryant, and I were having before-dinner drinks on the terrace. Hester came out, seating herself imperiously on a stone bench between the terrace and the swimming pool, said she was starved, and, just as José had predicted, announced she would stay for dinner.

For a brief unguarded instant, Elissa's eyes looked absolutely murderous. Then she covered and, putting on an air of gracious politeness she hardly could have felt, refused to be baited into a head-on row which was clearly what Hester was angling for.

The remaining time before dinner was largely taken up by Hester goadingly exercising her partial ownership rights in demanding answers to a dozen questions concerning the ongoing grape harvest. And with Elissa then smoothly replying to each before John or Bryant could, and using her far superior knowledge as a way of putting Hester down.

During all this, Lureen, looking tanned and stunningly beautiful in a light linen suit, maintained the same kind of Olympian remoteness John usually did, but occasionally broke into a faintly amused smile as her dark eyes flicked from one sparring woman to the other.

John's customary aloofness, on the other hand, had been replaced by a continual scowl that could only mean he was inwardly smoldering with anger. He sat with his broad muscular shoulders hunched forward, staring out over the vineyards beyond the pool, elbows on his knees, his big powerful hands locked together so hard his knuckles were white. I had the feeling that at any moment he would explode.

And I felt sorry for Bryant. He was unnaturally silent, his normally friendly face somber in its lack of expression, his eyes, most of the time, fixed on his unfinished glass of wine. I knew he was desperately uncomfortable. The only time he showed any emotion was when he caught me looking at him and gave me a fleeting and resigned smile.

José finally came out to announce dinner. As we all rose to go to the dining room, Lureen, with no explanation, suddenly said she'd pass. After saying a perfunctory good night to all, she went off upstairs with a kiss for Hester while virtually ignoring John. I found that odd, to say the least, but remembered what Bryant had said that morning about her attitude toward money and men. I glanced John's way. If he felt slighted, however, he wasn't showing it, although Elissa wore a look of slightly pained forbearance.

We went off to dinner, Hester sailing ahead, and I could

only think that Lureen had decided to leave before serious fireworks began. But nothing happened throughout the meal except that, like the proverbial calm before a storm, Hester lapsed into an almost unnatural silence.

It wasn't until we were back in the living room and José served coffee that it began. Hester, without any preliminaries, suddenly looked across at Bryant, seated next to me on the couch, and said, "Well?"

"Well what?"

"What did he say? You did tell him, didn't you?"

Bryant knew at once what she meant, for he instantly looked annoyed. But he played dumb, almost as though trying to signal her to be quiet. "Tell who what, Hester?" he said.

Hester smiled thinly. It wasn't a nice smile. "Tell *him*, Bryant." Rather than use John's name, she simply nodded her head in his direction. "And about what I told you Friday on the telephone."

Bryant took a deep exasperated breath. "No," he said. "I haven't discussed it with John."

"Why not?"

"Look, Hester," he began. "As I tried to explain when you phoned, it's out of the question. It's harvest time, we'll probably do well this year, and . . . "

He didn't get further. She waved a dismissing hand. "Nonsense. Perhaps you believe in playing roulette. I don't. One more disaster like last year and we've had it." She finally spoke directly to John. "We've had an offer. A substantial one."

John and Elissa exchanged quick looks, and Elissa said, "I don't think we're interested in any offer at this point, Hester."

She spoke quietly but John couldn't contain himself any longer.

"We damn well aren't," he burst out belligerently. "Right, Bryant?"

Hester ignored him and mentioned the name of the major

West Coast brewery the offer had come from. "It won't get any better than this," she said.

"Well, tell them to stick to their beer," John said. His face had become flushed and I could tell he was barely restraining his temper.

"They're offering more money, cash on the line, than you could ever make in this dump over the next fifty years at best," Hester insisted.

"We still aren't interested," Elissa said, "Nor are we interested in your becoming the eventual sole owner of the Abbaye."

Hester stared at her, then burst into an incredulous laugh that had a definitely false ring. "Me?"

Elissa's eyes were suddenly knives. "Yes, you. The brewery couldn't care less about owning a winery. Nor, if I've heard correctly, could the brewery's chairman, who you've apparently convinced should marry you after he sheds his wife of thirty years. He'll persuade his board to vote up the money, then turn this place over to you as a nice little wedding present, right? Well, get something straight, Hester, dear. You're moving into the Abbaye and this house over my dead body and that's that."

Hester looked at her, her expression pure venom. Then she turned to Bryant, "I think you'd better talk some sense into these two, because, like it or not, I plan to give the brewery an answer tomorrow and the answer is going to be yes."

At that, John finally blew. He jumped to his feet. "You're not telling anybody yes, because it's no, n-o! Now get that into your head and stop wasting any more of your time, or ours."

The color drained from Hester's face and her voice became a dangerous purr. "John, darling, I'm not wasting my time," she said. "I don't accept your no. I don't accept it and I don't have to, as you'll find out."

"You'll accept it, like it or not," John shouted. "The Abbaye can't be sold until the company's liabilities are greater than its assets or until all shareholders agree. Those are the stipulations of the will. Neither has happened yet. In fact the bank extended our credit today for another year."

Hester wasn't through, though. "Defending a last will and testament against a lawsuit can be long and very messy. And expensive."

John laughed harshly. "Sue to break Simon's will? You wouldn't stand a chance."

"Perhaps not," Hester conceded. "But whether I'd win or not is unimportant. What it will cost you, if I sue, that's what counts."

Bryant tried to calm things down. "Look, Hester, perhaps now is not the time to discuss this. It's late and we're all very tired and tense and—"

She cut him off. "And you want me to leave. Well, I'm not tired or tense and I'm not going to leave until I'm good and ready. I own a quarter of this place, don't forget."

I thought John was going to walk over and hit her but Hester was saved by the bell, so to speak. José appeared and murmured discreetly that I was wanted on the telephone. I excused myself and went to the little telephone alcove between the living room and the front hall. The caller was my workaholic lawyer daughter, Joanna, still at her midtown Manhattan office well after midnight, New York time, and checking on me to see if I'd survived the balloon rally in one piece. I assured her I had and we made a date for lunch for the end of the week. Then, eternally grateful for her interruption and the chance it brought me to escape, I retreated to my room figuring nobody would miss me.

Just as I came up onto the second-floor landing, Bryant and Elissa entered the hall below. I had known Bryant was cutting the weekend short. He had an important client flying in from Houston for an urgent Sunday meeting. I thought I ought to thank him for the wonderful tour he'd given me, but something told me not to go back down. He and Elissa were still talking about Hester's offer and it was none of my business. I heard him say, "I'm terribly sorry, Elissa. I should have warned you that the offer I told you about yesterday came from her. But I hoped to find some way of backing her off before John heard about it. I hardly wanted him so upset, or you, when you're both up to your necks with the harvest."

"Don't worry yourself, Bryant. It's all right."

"Are you sure? I can stay longer if you want."

"No. You'll need a good night's sleep for tomorrow and I can handle her, I promise you. And John, too, if she pushes him too hard."

They said good night. Bryant went out to his Ferrari and Elissa turned from the door and headed back to the living room.

I continued on to the Blue Room, almost bumping into Lureen as she came from her room to cross the hall for the master bathroom. Before I closed the door, I heard the hiss of the shower as she turned it on.

A series of events then took place which at the time seemed so unimportant that eventually, when required to, I had difficulty remembering them.

My room proved not much of a refuge because one set of windows looked down onto the terrace and, through the open French doors to the living room, I could clearly hear John and Hester continuing to row, with John twice ordering her to leave his house at once and with Hester refusing and threatening a lawsuit if he tried to eject her physically.

Eventually, she tired and did leave. And I heard her say with unnecessary sarcasm, "Don't bother to show me out. I know the way." And laugh. Several moments later there was the sound of her convertible starting and going up the driveway. Then silence finally prevailed.

I got ready for bed. I was tired. Every bone ached from my hiking about the vineyards. I'd hardly settled myself and opened the book I'd brought along when I heard, some distance away, what I thought was a woman screaming. The sound lasted only a few seconds, then silence again. Elissa was in the house, Hester was gone, Lureen was in the shower—there was no other women on the property that I knew of. I put it down to a night bird of some sort and began to read. After fifteen minutes or so, I felt overwhelmingly sleepy. I reached for the bedside light and remembered I again hadn't locked my door.

I got up. The key didn't turn all the way in the lock so I opened the door to see what was wrong and was slightly startled to find Lureen, in her bathrobe and with a towel around her head from washing her hair, just outside her own room. Before I could say anything, she went past me with a faint smile and a murmured "Good night" and went down the back stairs.

I could again hear the shower running in the master bath so John or Elissa must have come up. I gave up on the lock and put a conveniently small chair under the door handle. I went back to bed and then, almost immediately, heard a strange scraping sound from down on the terrace. It was as though something heavy was being dragged over the flagstones and for a moment I felt vaguely alarmed. But fatigue overtook me and by the time I fell asleep, I'd forgotten all about it.

6

I AWOKE RELATIVELY EARLY the next morning and I thought, at first, in my Manhattan apartment with the usual ever-present wail of police or fire sirens in the distance. But then I slowly realized where I was and when the only sounds I heard were birds singing, I dismissed the sirens as a dream.

But they weren't a dream. They were very real. When I came down at about eight-thirty and crossed the hall I looked through the open front door and was surprised to see several police cars, an ambulance, and a small crowd of men standing about the archway leading into the cloister. Every alarm bell in me sounded immediately. Then I saw Elissa appear from the cloister and come slowly down the gravel drive toward the house. Her shoulders were slumped, she moved like a sleepwalker, hands shoved deep in her jeans pockets, and my first thought was that something must have happened to John.

When she reached the front door, I was there to meet her. "Elissa, what is it?"

"Oh, God, Margaret, it's so awful. It's Hester."

It didn't really register for a moment. Hester had gone

home, hadn't she, as I was getting ready for bed? I'd heard her leave.

Elissa took a deep breath. "John had to identify her, or what they've been able to find so far. I couldn't let him face that alone, so I went with him. The workmen discovered her earlier this morning. They called Roland Grunnigen and he came and got John and John called the police."

"She's dead," I said a little stupidly.

"Oh, yes," Elissa answered. And her whole body shuddered.

"But how? When?" My mind leapt to a car accident. It would have happened on the other side of the big iron entrance gates, probably very close by. But wouldn't I have heard a crash?

Elissa said numbly, "The police think it happened last night, soon after she left here. They found her in the stemmer-crusher."

It took a moment for this to register; for me to remember the machine I had seen the day before, the powerful Archimedean screw at the bottom of the big steel hopper sunk in the floor of the old dormitory. I'd stood and watched it chew ruthlessly into bunches of grapes, tearing leaves and stalks away as it forced them through a small aperture into the grinding mechanism which would smash and pulp them into juice. I thought of Hester in the same machine, caught by the screw, and I suddenly felt sick.

"There's no earthly reason for her having been there," Elissa went on. "The police say she was either pushed or thrown into it." She covered here face with her hands, as though again seeing the gruesome sight. "They're having to disassemble the entire machinery to try to get out whatever they can."

I was too horrified to respond immediately. The police had to be right. Given Hester's arrogant sense of ownership, she might possibly have stopped when leaving and for some unknown reason gone to the stemmer-crusher. And, conceivably, in spite of a security rail around the hopper, she might have fallen in. But the start button I'd seen that morning on my tour was ten feet away; she could not have reached it to activate the murderous screw. Or would not have wanted to. Hester Seldridge was hardly the type to kill herself. She'd been murdered.

José appeared with a tray bearing coffee and brandy. He had been told what had happened and was terribly concerned for Elissa. "This will help, madam. Perhaps on the terrace."

We went there and sat silently while José poured black coffee and cognac together in a cup. She sipped and gave him a grateful smile. "Thank you, José. I'll be all right. Where's Miss Lureen?"

José pointed upstairs. "Mister Grunnigen came down and told her a few minutes ago when she was having coffee. She went straight up and locked herself in her room."

I glanced up at the windows next to mine above the terrace. They were shut, the blinds down. Regardless of how bad a mother Hester might have been and even if only an adoptive one, this had to be perfectly awful for her.

After José left, Elissa stared out at the vineyards a moment, then said, "I keep thinking something will suddenly make it all go away. But it isn't going to, I know that. The police say she tried to claw her way out of the hopper when the machinery started. They think whoever threw her in kept pushing her back down. They found pieces of a barrel stave with her hair and blood on it jammed in the mechanism."

The horror of it stopped me from asking anymore questions and we sat in silence. I tried not to picture the terror the woman must have experienced in her last moments. She had to have known what her fate would be when the screw finally seized her feet. And I tried not to think of the scream I'd heard and so blithely put down to a night bird.

Finally, John showed up. It was hard to tell how he felt. His face was devoid of any expression. He poured coffee and said, almost matter-of-factly, "They've rounded up all the pickers for questioning. They kept asking me why, if she was headed for home after dinner, she would have gone into the cloister, especially at that hour of night. Why indeed?''

"She must have surprised someone," Elissa said. "Seen a light and gone to look. What else?''

"Someone treating us to more sabotage?" John said. "That's what I told the police, anyway." He added, "Of course from their point of view everyone is suspect. When they get through with the Mexicans, poor devils, they'll start on all of us.''

"Us?" Elissa looked shocked, then indignant.

"Sure. Who else? You, me, Grunnigen, José, Alice, Bryant, all the office staff and regular workers. Especially me.''

"You? Nonsense. On what grounds?''

He shook his head. "The way Hester was, who had a better reason for seeing her gone than I? Especially after last night.''

"They don't know about last night and don't need to know," Elissa said. "After she left, you were with me. We tidied up and came upstairs." She paused, then added emphatically, "Together.''

John smiled thinly. "Forget it. Who ever believes what a wife says?''

He was right, I told myself. They didn't. Elissa could claim what she wished, but after Hester left there had been no other witnesses of any sort to John's actions except Lureen and me. She might be considered as biased as Elissa and all I could say, if ever asked, would be that I'd heard the shower running in their bathroom which didn't mean John was in it, or even in their bedroom. Elissa could have been the one showering and John could have been anywhere.

I was jarred from my thoughts by Elissa herself. She sat suddenly bolt upright, eyes wide. "John! I'd forgotten. The Merlot! How much have we lost?''

And I remembered Bryant telling me that the Bordeaux red wine they produced was a combination of several grapes, the Merlot variety an important one and the first to be harvested.

I looked at John. At first, he didn't answer. He was staring out over the vineyards where the early morning fog was beginning to lift and let the blue light of the sky and the gold of warm sunlight filter through. It was hard to match what had just happened with such a scene of peace. Nor with John's seemingly unruffled calm when he finally said, "We've lost everything we've crushed until now, and that's almost the whole crop. The Health Department has already sent an inspector up and we have to empty all the Merlot vats."

"All of them?"

"All of them."

Elissa stared at her husband with an unguarded expression in her eyes I couldn't quite fathom. Was it anger? Then an extraordinarily stubborn look came over her. "All right," she exclaimed. "We'll buy more Merlot, some that's already been crushed and is in fermentation at another winery. Somebody's bound to have an excess. And we'll leave it with them until we harvest the Cabernet Sauvignon."

John smiled faintly. "It may not be that simple. The inspector also said we have to take down all the pipelines to the vats, the crusher-stemmer as well, of course, and steam-sterilize everything."

"But that could take days!" Elissa cried. "It did when we were sabotaged with pesticides. All the rest of our grapes, even our Chardonnay, could rot on the vine."

Again, John didn't respond at once. He drained his coffee cup first, then stood up abruptly before he said, "Maybe not and certainly not if I can help it. You get busy and find us some Merlot. I'm going down to Napa."

"What for?" Elissa demanded.

"Pipe. I'm going to lay new lines. That will take far less time than making good the old ones."

"But John, it's Sunday."

"I'll roust somebody out." He laughed harshly. "I'll be damned if I'll let Hester be the one to ruin us."

He went off and I was surprised at the way he was taking

things. I thought, this was a different John than the haughty aloof Olympian I'd seen until then. He seemed almost to be enjoying the challenge the disaster presented. Could Hester's death have been such a relief to him as to offset even the tremendous new difficulties the Abbaye faced? I was surprised at Elissa, too. She appeared to have completely recovered from her horror at the way Hester had died and was suddenly all business.

Bryant arrived about an hour later, driving up from San Francisco. He stopped by the house first to see Elissa, who was already on the telephone trying to line up substitute Merlot.

I spoke to him, also, for a few minutes. I felt relieved at his being there, even if he seemed quite shaken and far less sanguine than his brother. "I don't know what will happen, now," he told me. "Banks aren't famous for their patience. They may just decide this place is hopelessly jinxed."

He headed up to the winery to supervise things in John's absence.

I was thus left on my own. I considered knocking on Lureen's door to see if she wanted anything or if I could not at least offer her sympathy. But I thought better of it. She hardly needed a stranger in her life at that moment. As the morning wore on, however, just sitting about the house became oppressive. Even though Hester didn't live there, her death seemed present in every room. I'd taken almost all the photographs I needed and had made notes on most of what Bryant had told me. I had enough for the photo-story I'd come to do, and logic dictated I should catch the first plane back to New York.

Logic, however, had never played much of a role with me where my getting involved with murder was concerned. Now was no exception, and I knew as I'd known ever since Elissa told me about the death of the poor Mexican worker that I wasn't going anywhere. Although Hester might have been the meanest, most obnoxious woman ever, the loss of her life was no less terrible than his and made getting to the bottom of things more imperative than ever. I planned to find every excuse possible to stay on at the Abbaye.

Where the two murders were connected, I wasn't sure. But it was difficult not to see them as being so and that sabotage might be the link. My thinking didn't go beyond that, however, and obviously needed to.

Right now, running would help, I knew. It always stimulates my mind and besides, I felt out of shape because I hadn't done my daily two miles in over a week. Nor had I played any tennis and I'd been eating far too liberally for a woman my age who tries to keep the figure she had in her thirties. I had my running clothes with me and, optimistically, I put them on and headed up the drive for the front gates. The fog had gone, the weather was blissfully clear and still cool, promising the most perfect of days. A mile up the quiet country road beyond the chapel and a mile back, I thought, I'll feel a different woman.

But it wasn't to be. There had just been a murder. The police had their own ideas about what every single person at the Abbaye could or could not do and I, as I was about to discover most unpleasantly, was no exception.

THERE WERE STILL SEVERAL POLICE CARS, the ambulance, and a group of men by the archway into the cloister as I came up the drive. I walked by, trying hard not to dwell too much on why they were there and keeping my eyes on the big wrought-iron front gates.

Just beyond them I could see two parked cars with several men standing about, one with a camera. I guessed they were reporters and that the police were barring the press from entering. That bothered me. I didn't want to face whatever questions they might have but I worried needlessly—the gates were as far as I got. Reaching them, I found my way was abruptly blocked by a uniformed police officer whose shoulder patch said he belonged to Napa County Sheriff's Department. He told me brusquely, in effect, that I wasn't going one foot farther. When I began to protest, a man in a very non-Californian dark business suit detached himself from the archway where he was conferring with two younger men—both wearing RayBan sunglasses, as if they were a parody of secret-service agents. He came over and I had my first confrontation with Chief Detective Andrew Bognor in charge of the Napa County Homicide Task Force.

About forty, he was stocky and balding, with a pasty pale face and thick lips. His eyebrows were thin sarcastic arches above slightly froggish eyes; he had unattractively large ear lobes, the sort of wide prominent teeth which made you wonder if they were real or not, and an ugly purplish mole on his forehead, close to his left temple. In a foretaste of things to come, he didn't introduce himself, or even say hello. He certainly didn't smile. He just said, "Who are you?"

I identified myself.

He said, "You're not to leave this property until you have my permission."

I, then, had the temerity to ask him why on earth not.

"You were here last night?"

"Yes."

"Anybody on this property last night is suspect of murder or being an accessory to it. You'll be questioned later. You will be made aware of your rights and you may have a lawyer present if you wish."

I caught my breath and found my tongue. "Wait a minute, Officer, I didn't even know the poor woman. I'm just a journalist here to do a story. I came Friday night."

"You'll be given a chance to explain all that in due course."

"When is 'in due course'?"

He didn't answer. He turned on his heel and rejoined his group. I considered going after him—at that time I still hadn't learned his name—then thought better of it. He wasn't the sort of man, I was certain, who would yield to persuasion. I went back to the house, changed into a cool summer dress, and tried to think what I should do.

I debated, first off, calling my daughter to make certain of my legal rights. It was already well past lunchtime in New York and, knowing Joanna, I envisioned her having a Sunday sandwich at her desk on the forty-fourth floor of her office building. She, I knew, would instantly put me in touch with the California branch of her law firm. I decided against it. Joanna became impossibly bossy whenever I was involved in anything she thought wasn't right for me, and I was not in the mood to be ordered around by my own child as though I were a twelve-year-old. Besides, the unattractive, bullying Bognor hadn't yet questioned me. When he did, I reassured myself, he'd soon see how ridiculous it was to bother with me.

At noon, when still not called upon to face the Law, I took my camera with a telephoto lens, as well as a book and some sandwiches José provided, out to the vineyards for an early lunch of my own. From a vantage point looking down at the winery I could see the courtyard with a certain amount of police activity going on. Men were measuring, dusting doorways for fingerprints, photographing. I got some interesting shots I thought might liven up another story on a winery later on, then settled beneath an olive tree to enjoy my book and sandwiches.

I'd pulled a bunch of grapes from a neighboring vine for dessert when I was startled by a shadow falling over me. Looking up, I found myself confronted by the same sour-faced uniformed sheriff's officer who'd blocked my path to the entrance gates. He was accompanied by one of the slick young men who had been talking to Bognor earlier. This younger man carried a clipboard with what I presumed was a list of names, and, after looking down at it, grinned unpleasantly and asked, "Mrs. Barlow?"

I nodded and he jerked a thumb at the winery. "Chief Detective Bognor will see you now."

The arrogance of it made me angry. I looked from one man to the other. Clipboard produced another nasty smile and said nothing. The officer had a face like stone. I decided to keep my temper to myself and rose and followed both men. At least I had learned the name of my persecutor.

Crossing the cloister to the office entrance, two ambulancemen wearing rubber gloves came out from where the hopper was located, each carrying small tagged plastic bags which they carefully placed in the back of their vehicle. I turned my head away quickly.

Bognor had installed himself in Hester's office. His first

words to me when I was ushered into his presence were, "You may have a lawyer present if you wish."

When I told him I didn't think I needed one, he read me my rights and, poising a silver pencil over a pad of legal foolscap, began firing questions at me: name, age, residence, when I'd come to the Abbaye and why. I reminded him that I was a journalist and when it emerged that I was freelance a faint smug smile crossed his face. Clearly, that was something in his book hardly worthy of mention and thus slightly suspect.

"And how long have you known Mrs. Seldridge?"

"Just since I arrived."

"Not during her film career?"

"No."

"And Mr. Seldridge?"

"The same. Since Friday."

"And how long were you acquainted with the deceased?"

"I didn't know her at all. We were barely introduced yesterday."

"You have no financial interest in these vineyards or the wine produced here?"

"None whatsoever."

I could see he didn't believe me and guessed he was going to check out everything I said. Well, good luck, I thought.

He made notes, making me wait for what seemed forever, then asked me to tell him everything I could remember of the previous evening. I did so and as accurately as I could. At first I planned to avoid mentioning the row between John and Hester. I didn't like being cast as an informer. But I decided I'd better not since he'd probably learn of it from someone else, José, for instance, and it would look as though I were covering up something. So I termed the bitter scene a disagreement and played down John's anger.

"They fought?"

"I didn't say that. No, not at all."

"Threatened?"

"No."

"What was the argument about?"

I said I wasn't quite sure but thought it had to do with whether the property should be sold or not.

"She was his former wife, am I right?"

"I believe so, yes."

"You didn't find her coming to dinner a little strange?"

I shrugged. "She was part-owner of the winery," I said. "I guess they had business to discuss."

"Business, yes. But dinner?"

I agreed but I wasn't about to let him know. "Some people manage to be civilized," I said.

He grunted disbelief, glanced at his notes, then asked me other questions. After Hester left for home, where were all the family? I told him Lureen was in the shower getting ready to retire, John and Elissa I thought were first putting the house to bed and then had come upstairs themselves. I heard them in the bathroom, I said. I didn't voice the vague suspicions I'd had that Elissa could have been alone in their bedroom and bathroom, and John anywhere else. Let him do his own suspecting. But he jumped on it.

"Both of them?"

"I wasn't with them," I said. He let it go but made a note and I told him, then, of the scream I'd heard and put down to a night bird and that later I'd seen Lureen going down the back stairs.

"Before or after you heard the scream?"

"After." My patience was getting thin by then and I couldn't help but feel sorry for Lureen. I doubted whether Bognor would care that she'd just lost her mother and in the most awful way imaginable. I was sure he'd put her through a similar grilling. I added, tartly, "She'd just come out of the shower."

His next question caught me completely off-guard. He wrote something on his pad, making me wait, and then, without looking up, said, "Does the name Julio Garcia-Sanchez mean anything to your?" It didn't but it was easy to guess whom he meant

"I'm not sure," I answered. "Was he the hit-and-run victim?"

He smiled thinly. "You claim it was hit-and-run?"

"I don't claim anything. I don't even know if I'm thinking of the right person. I understand that there was a Mexican migrant worker killed on the road the other night."

His answer was another question. "Where were you that night, Mrs. Barlow?"

I began to feel I was living a bad dream. Could this horrid little man possibly be trying to connect me with the unfortunate grape picker? "Probably," I said, "after ten o'clock, asleep in my motel room in Sonoma."

"In your motel room," he repeated. "Do you have anyone who can confirm that?"

"I doubt it," I said, as acidly as I could. "I'm traveling alone."

He studied his notes again and then said I could go. "We'll want a complete record of all your activities since you came to California. Including names of everyone you were involved with. And, including your time alone." He almost sneered over the word. "Be prepared to give it."

And that was the first time he had me genuinely worried. I could see him hounding my ballooning hosts. I said, and I admit facetiously, "All right. I don't have to leave for the airport until this evening."

He took me seriously. "Airport?" he snapped. "You're not going to any airport. You're not leaving California."

I think I simply stared at him. My eyes seemed to fix, embarrassingly, on the large purplish mole on his forehead. Being told I couldn't leave didn't upset me since I planned to stay anyway. But uppermost in my mind was the thought that I wasn't going to be let off with only one session like this, that I was in for a lot more, in fact was due to be investigated as intensely as though I were one of the Seldridges or a winery employee.

I didn't relish the idea at all. I decided to pretend I really did have plans to leave and see how far I could push him. "Look, Officer . . ."

"Chief Detective Bognor," he corrected. His smile was less friendly than ever.

"Sorry. Detective Bognor, then. My being here when this murder occurred is entirely coincidental. I've told you absolutely everything I can. Now, please, if you should need me again, which I doubt, I'm sure you could always telephone me in New York or have me deposed, if you wished."

He didn't trouble himself to answer me. Instead and without looking up from the several pages of notes he'd made, he said, "Tell me about Mr. Seldridge."

That caught me off-balance. What now? "Seldridge? Which Mr. Seldridge?"

"Bryant Seldridge. I want to know about your personal relationship with him."

The insinuation was pretty clear and I almost couldn't believe it. "If you mean what I think you mean," I snapped, "I don't have one."

"You never met him before you came here?"

"No."

"How about Mr. Grunnigen, then?"

This was so absurd, I laughed. I couldn't help it. "The young man who works here?"

Bognor didn't think it funny, though. His eyes hardened and his voice became nearly a hiss. "Yes, Mrs. Barlow. Roland Grunnigen. Do you also claim you've never been intimate with him?"

That did it. I boiled over. "Look here, mister," I said, "One more question like that and you'll get your smug face slapped. Police officer or no."

He looked up. And flushed a deep red. "I would like to remind you, madam," he said in a choked voice, "that on behalf of the Napa County Sheriff, I am conducting an investigation into a murder. You can either answer my questions here in this office or answer them in a cell in the county jail." He looked away from me and called out, "Corporal?"

The stone-faced officer appeared in the doorway. Bognor smiled. "The lady is making up her mind whether to stay here or go with you to Napa City."

I sat in silence a moment, debating with myself how best to handle this. All right, I thought, he's a despicable bully but you've obviously underestimated just how despicable as well as his authority to carry out his threat if you don't retreat. And quickly. County jail is definitely not where you want to be, so forget pride, for the moment at least, and let him think he's succeeded in cowing you.

"Well?" He tapped his pencil impatiently.

I surrendered with what I thought was a suitable display of defeat. "Okay," I said "You're the boss. The answer is no."

He leaned back in his chair, enjoying his victory. "You see, Mrs. Barlow? That wasn't so difficult was it?" He shuffled the notes he'd made into a folder."Show Mrs. Barlow back to the house," he said to the officer. It was the first time he deigned to call me by my name.

"Thank you," I said. And then, hiding how I felt about him as best I could, asked him the sixty-four-dollar question. "Am I allowed to know on what grounds you're keeping me in California?"

"Oh, I suspect we can find 'grounds' easily enough *Mrs*. Barlow. If you want us to formalize them. Material witness, obstructing justice, suspicion of murder." His smile was one I'd just as soon forget. "Threatening bodily harm to a police officer."

I felt Stone-Face's hand on my arm.

Going downstairs to the cloister, I vaguely realized I'd forgotten to tell him of the strange scraping sound I'd heard on the terrace below my window. I didn't care. Somewhere during Bognor's questioning, I'd begun to have an overwhelming desire to cut him down to size and the best way to do that, I knew, was to unmask Hester's and the Mexican's murderer or murderers before he did. If the scraping sound should ever turn out to be important, it would be one point to my advantage.

When the officer had deposited me at the front door, I headed straight for the back terrace. I'd enjoy the early afternoon sun, I decided, have a glass of wine to get the bad taste of Bognor out of my mouth, and think.

José appeared in the hall. "José?"

"Madam?"

"Some ice-cold white wine for me, please," I said. "Out there." I pointed toward the terrace.

José grinned. "Yes, madam. I had vodka after I was questioned." He giggled and I realized he'd probably had more than one.

I laughed. "Wine will do," I said, and went on.

If I thought to sit quietly by myself, however, I was mistaken. As I came through the French doors into the sun, a man rose from a chair to greet me. He was the most extraordinary little man, too. I say little because I doubt he was much taller than five foot three. He was past seventy, I guessed, although later I learned to my utter astonishment that he was eighty-three, and he looked like a cherub with an airy cloud of snowy white hair. Positively pear-shaped, he wore a severely rumpled blue-and-white striped seersucker suit, an equally rumpled pink shirt adorned with an outrageous necktie sporting a hand-painted explicitly naked girl on roller skates, socks to match his shirt, and sandals.

Seeing me, his cherubic face broke into a smile of pleasure. He rushed forward, looked up at me, stuck out his hand to be shaken, and announced, "Ah, Margaret Barlow, I'm certain. Aubrey Cloudsmith, at your service."

8

Rather bewildered, I said, "How do you do?" to which his response was "Excellent, my dear. Couldn't fare better. I've got the best news story I've had since the Highway 29 strangler. Did in seven hitchhikers before they caught up to him. Surely you remember. Men and women. Made no difference to him. A neck was a neck. He was a vintner from Sonoma, quite respected in those parts, too. He'd take them home to his winery, fill them up with Pinot Noir until they were in seventh heaven, then throttle them off to the real place."

I found myself vaguely remembering the murders some ten years before. Simultaneously, I realized that this was "the media" and wondered how on earth he'd managed to get into the Abbaye, to say nothing of ensconcing himself on the private terrace of the owners when the police were plainly barring entry to other reporters.

As though reading my thoughts, he flourished a business card in my direction and I read:

C. Aubrey Cloudsmith
Editor in Chief
The Valley Recorder

And heard him say, "We cover Sonoma and the northern Central Valley and Sierra wine regions also."

I looked up. Or perhaps down. "How did you get in here?" I demanded. That's when I noticed, on a table, the big Speed Graflex camera, the kind that for years was standard with every news photographer. It looked as though it had seen a century of use.

He was clearly delighted to tell me. "Easy," he declared. "Bognor owed me one. And I've known John Seldridge since he first appeared on earth." Without further ado, he plunked himself down in a chair, inviting me cordially, as if he owned the Abbaye, to do the same. "Do sit down, my dear, we have a lot to talk about."

"Sorry," I said at once, "I'm afraid I only arrived Friday and you surely know more about what's happened than I."

"Oh, please, please," the little man expostulated, throwing up his hands. "I quite understand. You've barely had time to settle in. All I'd like to talk about is you."

"Me?"

"Yes, you. Indeed."

"There's nothing interesting about me," I returned. "I'm simply a weekend guest who's now stuck here, apparently."

"Stuck here. Exactly. Bognor's got you grounded, has he? Typical. And just what I thought. Which is exactly the reason for our partnership to be."

"Partnership?" I echoed. I didn't quite know whether to laugh or not.

"Exactly," he repeated. "You and I."

A strange thing then happened. The eccentric little cherubic man, as though simply camouflage, abruptly disappeared to be replaced by a steely-eyed, no-nonsense professional newspaper editor. Even the voice changed.

"Now look," he said. "Bognor sees you, until he's proved wrong, as a possible material witness, if not a suspect. Ridiculous, of course, but there you are. And if I know Bognor, which I do, he'll keep you hanging about until he has the murderer under lock and key. That could be this afternoon.

tomorrow, or . . ." he paused significantly " . . . next year. Who knows? In the strangler case he kept one poor fellow here in California for months on one charge after another and when the man fled the state eventually got him extradited. So what our partnership will be is this—I will supply you with accurate inside information as to what progress the police are making, notably with their forensic efforts, and you will use that information coupled with your own investigative talents to solve the murder. Then, *ecco*, I get your exclusive story for my paper and you fly off to New York. Agreed?"

This time, I did laugh. "I don't think so," I said. "What on earth makes you think I'm capable of investigating anything, let alone murder? I'm not a detective. And how do you know I live in New York?"

"I know a great deal about you, Mrs. Barlow. But first, I am well aware you are not a detective, and thank heaven for that. In my experience, detectives are rather limited in imagination and thus often in success. You're not just a very pretty woman, either; you're a very good photo-journalist. Oh, don't say no to a little honest flattery. I've seen a half-dozen articles by you in various magazines. Several have been virtually pure investigative reporting. You have a great intuitive facility for ferreting out things, as it were. And then, of course, there's my colleague on the *Baltimore Sun*."

"Oh," I said. I began to understand.

He smiled slyly. "Yes, indeed, Brides Hall, the snobby girls boarding school on the Eastern Shore of Maryland. He covered the goings-on there for his paper. And then there was an item or two in the *Boston Globe*."

Item? There'd been a full page at least. So much for my telling him I'd never investigated murder. "Martha's Vineyard," I confessed.

"Exactly. Murder most foul there, too, my dear. One poor innocent fed to snapping turtles, another throttled by a cranked-up car window. A third handily run through with a pitchfork."

An alarm bell began to sound in the back of my head. "I hope," I said, "that you haven't gone and divulged any of this to Bognor."

"Oh, good Heavens, no. Our chief detective has a positive compulsion to think he's the sole person capable of doing anything. The slightest whisper and he'd see you as such a threat he'd probably find any excuse possible to lock you up on the spot."

The little man rose, retrieved a broad-brimmed panama hat from where he'd tossed it onto a chair, and as fast as he had disappeared, the flowery little cherubic man reappeared again. "Of course you must have time to think it over, Margaret, my dear. I do understand. I wouldn't expect you to do otherwise. Not you. You have my card. Give me a call. Meanwhile, let me say it's been most delightful meeting you and I do hope you'll be able to get to the bottom of things quickly. I could use a scoop. And you will want to clear things up, too, as soon as possible," he added. "I'm sure you will."

With that, he wished me good day, raised the panama high above his head in an old-fashioned gesture of courtesy, and hastened off, looking for all the world like a scurrying blue-and-white toadstool.

It took me a few moments to collect myself. José finally appeared with an ice-cold bottle of 1982 Chardonnay, and that helped.

"Do you know Mr. Cloudsmith, José?"

"Oh, yes. Everyone knows Mr. Cloudsmith." He smiled broadly but didn't offer any more.

I finished a glass of wine and then began to seriously consider what Cloudsmith had said about Bognor. It was hardly encouraging. I wasn't so worried about how long the homicide detective might want to keep me in California. Back east, I had a story to do on an end-of-the-season yachting regatta and my Martha's Vineyard home to put to bed for the winter, but I felt confident I could get to the bottom of things myself before time finally ran out on me. If Cloudsmith were right, however, and Bognor had me locked up for invading his turf and then was unable to turn up the murderer, I could find myself a guest of the Napa County sheriff for longer than I cared to imagine.

I was thinking along those lines and reaching for the wine bottle to fill my glass when Lureen, to my surprise wearing a short terrycloth beach robe, appeared in the doorway to the living room and came out onto the terrace. I rose to offer my condolences but had hardly begun when she stopped me cold and with an indulgent smile, said, "Thanks, Mrs. Barlow," and proceeded straight on to the pool.

What she did next left me speechless. Perhaps I'm old-fashioned, but somehow the acceptable swimwear for young women all around the Mediterranean didn't fit in with my idea of a daughter in mourning. Lureen went to a canvas chaise lounge by the pool and, as casually as though on the beach at St. Tropez, took off her robe to reveal her beautiful muscular young body in total suntanned nudity except for the smallest bottom half of a string bikini. Poor little José came out again at that moment to tidy up a bit. He quickly averted his eyes and fled back inside.

On her part, Lureen seemed completely indifferent to his momentary presence—and to mine. She wasn't flaunting herself, I realized; it was simply that both José and I were of so little importance to her that we virtually didn't exist. She rubbed suntan oil all over herself and then lay on her back on the chaise lounge.

And I quelled an urge to go over and tip the chaise lounge into the pool.

Ironically, for me the fact that she seemed to ignore the horror of her mother's murder somehow made it twice as awful. Even though I had no sympathy for him, I put myself in Bognor's shoes, and began to understand a little of why he was being so hard-nosed. Because of the way Hester was murdered and the importance and glamour of the wine business, there would be a demand for his success in tracking down the killer where there had been no interest at all in poor Julio Garcia-Sanchez. If anyone at the Abbaye, myself included, were not suspected and thoroughly investigated and then later found to be either guilty or a valuable material witness, Bognor's career would be ruined.

The chief detective could turn out to be a worse adversary than I'd thought. I was going to have to be very careful not to cross him.

9

HESTER'S FUNERAL was two days later. A brief service in a rather cold and sterile modern church near Sonoma was followed by a perfunctory burial of her coffined remains in a nearby cemetery.

Marred by a chill morning fog that had swept up from San Francisco Bay, it was attended only by a handful of friends; by Lureen, who hid her face and eyes behind a dark veil and was the only person to wear mourning; and by John, Elissa, and Bryant.

"It won't look right if we're not there," Elissa told me the evening before. "After all we *were* in business with her, she *did* die at the Abbaye and probably because of it, and she *was* Lureen's mother."

I attended because the more I involved myself with everything concerning the Abbaye, the more I knew I would develop an intuitive feeling about the people and the place that would help me to get to the bottom of things.

Bognor was there, too, a dark and unattractive figure who hung about expressionless in the background along with his two assistants in their secret-service sunglasses, making everyone even more uncomfortable than they already were. What he hoped to achieve, I don't know. Perhaps he misguidedly thought one of us would somehow betray guilt through lack of grief, in which case, nearly all of us must have satisfied him.

And Aubrey Cloudsmith also attended. He avoided me but he caught my eye once and winked. He had changed his clothes for the event and looked altogether respectable.

Conspicuously absent was Hester's wealthy brewery chairman and lover. Neither he nor any of Hester's friends had volunteered to make the final arrangements, and the unwanted task had fallen on the shoulders of poor Alice Brooks.

"Back to his wife in a hurry is my guess," Bryant muttered as we stood near the yawning graveside.

Afterward, we all returned to the Abbaye and I drove with Bryant in his Ferrari. We almost ran into Bognor as we came out through the cemetery gates and Bryant laughed. "Locking fenders with him is all I need, though he has to be at least polite with us because the Napa County sheriff is a close friend of mine."

He glanced in his rear-view mirror at Bognor's car behind us and accelerated away. "The problem with our chief detective," he went on, "is that he's one of those people who are never satisfied with the obvious, and the obvious in this case is that as she drove to the front gate, Hester surprised someone in yet another act of sabotage. We'll never know for sure, of course, but the odds are that she saw a light in the cloister and, Hester being Hester, she stopped to see what was going on. It would have been just like her to do so. If anybody was actually tampering with the crusher-stemmer, he would have found the machine a quick and easy way to get rid of her as a witness."

Bryant shook his head in disgust. "But that's too cut and dry for Bognor. He's got to wallow around looking for some more devious motive, and ridiculously suspecting everyone, you included, I hear, as well as John, Elissa, and me as though we needed to inflict ourselves with yet another disaster."

But even as he talked and in spite of the common sense of what he said, a nagging voice at the back of my mind kept saying that it might not be as simple as Bryant believed, that there could be more behind Hester's death than the Mexican's. A saboteur killing her to hide his identity could be just what someone wanted Bryant and everyone else to believe. Perhaps it was John who made me think so. I kept having a strange feeling that he knew more about the murders, Hester's anyway, than he was saying. As we walked away from the grave, I was sure I'd seen a faint smile cross his face.

"What about the alarm system?" I asked. "How would a saboteur get past it? Surely it must have some sort of an anti-tamper device? Most alarms do."

"It does," Bryant replied, "and it's something that's always puzzled everyone for the past two years. Either someone knows how to overcome the anti-tamper system—and that's possible but only if they're a real pro—or we're dealing with an inside job, one of our trusted employees either doing the sabotaging himself or being paid by someone outside to shut down the alarm so they can. An employee is the more likely possibility. And the nastiest."

We arrived back at the Abbaye and Bryant, who had to attend a meeting in San Francisco, dropped me off at the house before he went up to the winery office to collect some papers he'd left there. "If Bognor gets too heavy-handed with you," he said, "let me know. I'll have a word with the sheriff, although, if I know Bognor, the best approach is no approach. You don't want him to get his back up any more than he has and have him formalize charges against you, so you're actually better off at the moment without even breathing the word lawyer."

I thanked him and told him not to worry about me, that I thought I could handle Bognor.

"Given what's happened, Bognor might be the least of your worries, Margaret," he cautioned before he drove off. "Be careful around this place."

I promised him I would and joined John and Elissa, who had come down the drive right behind us.

We had just stepped through the front door when José met us in the hall with the whispered information that a visitor was awaiting us on the terrace—Harry Charwood. Elissa laughed and even John smiled. He shook his head. "The first of the vultures," he said. We all went out to the terrace.

I don't know what my image of Charwood was before I met him—some sort of a sinister gangster with an appearnance to match John's calling him a vulture, I suppose. Whatever, it was completely erased by the man I met. When he reared cumbersomely to his feet from half-reclining in a chair with a bottle of champagne nearly hidden in a hand that resembled a Virginia ham, I had the immediate impression of a plantation owner in some far away place like Malaysia. What stood up was a great sweating hill of beef with not a vulture's scrawny neck but a thick bull neck and not a vulturous beak face but a huge red moon sporting a bushy mustache as flaming orange as a last fringe of hair separating his ears from a sunburned bald pate. He was in his midfifties I guessed, well over six feet, weighed about two hundred and fifty pounds, and wore vast baggy work trousers and a white shirt open to his waist to show off several medallions hung about his neck by gold chains.

"Ah, there you are," he bellowed at John. "Bluebeard himself. Gave her the push, did you Seldridge?"

This was followed by a great shout of laughter and then, before either John or Elissa could answer or even think of introducing me, he waved his champagne bottle in my direction. "And who is this pretty little co-conspirator?"

I was introduced. John nodded at the champagne bottle and commented that Charwood seemed to have found something to drink.

"Brought my own, Seldridge. In deference to your current financial chaos. And to celebrate my finally buying you out."

Elissa told Charwood he was incorrigible and that they weren't selling. José, as though on cue, had arrived with more champagne and Charwood knocked back two glasses of it in seconds. He then offered John a sum for the Abbaye which was a great deal of money. John was quick to point out that this was half what the property was worth and Charwood was equally quick to respond.

"But you've no choice, young man," he thundered. "You're cornered. And the whole valley knows it. You were up to your proverbial neck in bank loans even before your 'ex' exited."

He paused to roar laughter over his own play on words, and then added, "You can hope some of our mutual and esteemed colleagues will make you a better offer, of course, but I doubt they will. And I'll pay cash, remember. No shilly-shallying around with silly banks and their damned mortgages. Just a large suitcase full of good old greenbacks."

It went on like that until all the champagne was finished. Charwood finally departed with an admonishment to John to "Think it over, young man. Sleep on it and call me in the morning. Before the banks call you." And an invitation to me to "Come down to my place, young lady, anytime. I've tons of champagne in my cellar, the best. It came with the joint when I bought it, and it's just waiting to be opened."

"Give our regards to Jaconello," Elissa said with a cryptic smile.

Charwood stopped dead in midstride. There was a moment's silence. He turned, stared and then bellowed a final laugh. "Jaconello? Jaconello? Never met the man! Wouldn't know him if I fell over him. And what would he possibly want with a poor grape grower like me, anyway?"

As he went through the living room, we could hear him offering José a job as his major domo when he eventually owned the Abbaye.

Elissa let out a sigh of relief and I asked if the Jaconello they mentioned was *the* Jaconello.

"One and the same," she replied.

I don't think there was anyone who hadn't heard of Alfonse Jaconello. With a fortune made in high finance piracy, the Swiss-born billionaire had plundered the world of art treasures to garnish the palace he had built himself in the Sierra Madre mountains on the central California coast.

"We suspect Harry Charwood is fronting for him," Elissa continued. "Harry hardly has enough money of his own to buy anything, let alone this place, and Jaconello has tried everything else. He offered personally to buy us out several years ago and we told him to get lost. I guess that drove him half-crazy. Apparently nobody had ever told him no before. He doubled his offer, sent teams of his lackeys to see us. The answer has always been no."

"And you think he takes no as being personally directed at just him?"

"Yes," Elissa replied. "He's a man who simply can't believe anyone could ever refuse money because he places such a huge importance on it himself. So he seems to have decided we have something against him personally. Hence a front man."

"But why on earth would he want a winery?" I asked. "He has enough money to buy half the wine in France as well as here."

Elissa laughed. "We suspect revenge," she said. "Most people don't know it but he started in wine. His family owned a small vineyard above Lake Geneva. They made good money, enough to send Jaconello to Oxford, then to business school in America. But he never forgot his roots or that when he was a boy, French vintners used to laugh at the inferior wine his family produced. He's always wanted to get back at them with the finest vintage in the world, and he wouldn't need more acres than the ones we already produce from."

I didn't get a chance to learn more because José returned with news that they were about to receive another visit. It was a veteran vintner as renowned for his neighborliness and generosity as he was for the excellent wines he produced. He was coming to discuss selling the Abbaye some desperately needed Merlot.

I left John and Elissa talking business with him while I changed to go running. This time I was untroubled by the police or by the big wrought-iron front gates which opened easily and quietly when I pointed the little pocket transmitter at them which Elissa had provided me with earlier.

The road, winding between hills covered with groves of pine and oak, was traffic-free. The sky was clear, the sun warm, birds sang; here and there in the woods off the road, I saw clumps of lovely wildflowers. It all seemed so very innocent compared to the dark happenings at the Abbaye. Two acts of sabotage, two vicious murders; the police apparently with no leads at all but enter now a clown perhaps masterminded by a billionaire puppeteer, for I didn't believe for one instant that Harry Charwood was the innocent buffoon he seemed to be. Yet, at the same time, I told myself he seemed a little too obvious a candidate for my liking to be the saboteur and murderer I sought. What was he up to, then? Was he indeed fronting for Jaconello? Somehow Elissa's suspicion he was didn't ring true to me.

I returned to the Abbaye to hear a triumphant Elissa tell me that she and John had successfully negotiated a deal to replace the vital Merlot wine they'd lost because of Hester. I congratulated her but my thoughts were elsewhere. I had a growing number of questions I didn't have answers for, and I needed to know, also, what Bognor was up to. The person who could best help me, I decided, was C. Aubrey Cloudsmith. I was determined to contact him as soon as possible.

10

I CALLED the old news editor first thing in the morning. He
expressed delight at our "partnership in the realm of crime,"
a paraphrase that made me wince, and we arranged to meet
at five o'clock in the chapel, a place, I'd decided, we'd be
least likely to be disturbed either by Bognor's homicide squad
or the Seldridges.

At ten, Bryant came up from San Francisco accompanied
by Hester's lawyer, who read her will. We all gathered in
the living room for the occasion, including Lureen, of course.

There were no surprises. As apparently required by Simon's will, Hester left Lureen her one-quarter share of the
Abbaye. Strangely, she made no mention of her personal
effects or a house on San Francisco's Nob Hill which had
belonged first to old Simon Seldridge, then to John, and
which the divorce court had awarded to her. It was almost
as though Lureen didn't exist, but Bryant said that although
it would take a little time, it would go to Lureen automatically as her mother's sole survivor and heir.

Uppermost in my mind during the proceedings was that
nothing had changed in the ownership of the Abbaye except
that Lureen had now officially entered the picture. She could

agree to a sale of the Abbaye or block it, and that gave her a lot of leverage where Elissa was concerned. I wondered how long it would be before trouble broke out because of it. I'd already seen the friction that existed between Elissa and her.

Shortly before five, I set off for my meeting with Cloudsmith. John had worked night and day readying the wine-making machinery and the health department had finally given the Abbaye a clean bill. They had started harvesting the Cabernet Sauvignon and the cloister was a bustle of activity, with the crusher-stemmer swallowing up grapes from a gondola as I entered. The winery was no longer off-limits, and to my relief, a uniformed officer watching the proceedings hardly glanced at me. Nor did one of Bognor's assistants who appeared, as sinister as ever in his business suit and sunglasses, in the entrance to the cuvier.

I entered the chapel through the vestry, a small, dusty, once white-washed room, the door to which was at the end of the stone-columned loggia running along one side of the courtyard. It took me a moment to adjust my eyes to the gloom in the chapel itself and I didn't see Cloudsmith at first. When he spoke my name from close by, I nearly jumped out of my skin. I spun about and still saw no one, until the little man, wearing the most pixieish of grins, rose from where he was waiting on the steps to the altar with his old Speed Graflex camera and where I saw, to my surprise, a wine bottle and two large silver chalices I'd noticed before on the altar itself.

He waved the bottle and said, "I took the liberty while you were evading the law out there to fetch a coolish Chardonnay from the crypt below. I'm sure John would not begrudge us a little for a good cause."

He produced a waiter's corkscrew from a baggy pocket and opened the bottle, filling the two chalices. Raising his in toast, he said, "Your health, dear lady, and the success of our venture." His flowery pixie front then disappeared the way it had before, replaced by the steely-eyes newsman. "I saw Harry Charwood down in the valley," he added. "He said he'd made an offer and got turned down, as usual."

I told him about the visit and asked if he had known Charwood long.

"I met him when he first came here fifteen years ago," he answered. "Nobody quite knows from where. He said his mother had left him some money; she was an art dealer of sorts, apparently. He worked around the valley a spell getting to know the ropes of wine-making and then, a few years back, bought the vineyard at the bottom of the hill."

"How much of his buffoonery do you think is a front?"

"Shrewd of you, Margaret. Most of it, I'd say."

"Who's the real Charwood, then?"

"Hard to tell. Harry keeps pretty much to himself. Doesn't socialize."

"Do you think him capable of sabotage and murder?"

Cloudsmith was thoughtful a moment. Then he said, "Sabotage, yes, perhaps. If he was paid enough. Murder? I'm not sure. But he might be off both hooks, anyway."

"Oh? Why is that?"

There was a hint of triumph in the old editor's tone at knowing something I hadn't yet learned. "As of this morning," he declared, "Bognor has pretty much ruled out any saboteur or outsider as the person we seek."

That was news, all right. "Why?" I asked.

"It seems that our Hester had a planned rendezvous with someone at the winery after she left the Seldridge's house. She drove out through the front gates and then around to the employees' parking lot." He nodded at the far side of the chapel. "Out there. She left her car and came back into the Abbaye through here, then the vestry and out into the loggia. Forensic found traces of parking-lot dust on one of her shoes that didn't go down into the crusher-stemmer with her."

While I absorbed this new information, Cloudsmith waved

a notebook he extracted from a jacket pocket. "She telephoned while shopping with Lureen to leave a message on her brewery chairman's personal answering machine."

"Bognor, I presume," I said, "got on to him during a routine examination of personal effects and papers in her home."

Cloudsmith smiled. "Clever young lady. And she was surprisingly indiscreet." He thumbed through some smudged pages until he came upon what he was looking for. "Ah, here we are. 'Darling, it's me. Don't wait up. I may be very late. I'm meeting my person at the winery after dinner. I'll call you first thing in the morning. Good night.' "

"And the brewer didn't say who that person was?" I demanded, slightly incredulous.

Cloudsmith shook his head. "Afraid not. He told Bognor Hester had boasted for some time that she had someone she could pressure to make the Seldridges sell. But she refused to reveal who it was until she closed the deal."

I poured us both some more wine to give myself a chance to think. My first reaction was to wonder if Hester wasn't the person behind the sabotage. It certainly sounded so and I wouldn't have put it past her. But I'd hardly had the thought when Cloudsmith said, "The brewer was very firm that she'd had nothing to do with the sabotage. On the contrary, he said that when he himself had jokingly accused her of it because it helped put the pressure on the Seldridges, especially John, she'd become very angry with him. She'd insisted she'd had nothing to do with it at all. She didn't need to take that kind of risk, she'd said."

And she didn't, I thought. Not for more wealth, anyway. She was already rich and her brewer hardly poor. My thoughts now thoroughly jolted, I summed up what I'd heard. I felt a little chagrined that Bognor had clearly beaten me to the punch. I hadn't got further than not quite trusting the saboteur caught-in-the-act theory Bryant had accepted as gospel. Bognor had and the implication was that Hester might well have been murdered premeditatively by whomever she was supposed to meet.

A finger thus pointed at someone inside the Abbaye as being that person. For if an outsider, why risk having that someone come out to the Abbaye when she could easily have met them somewhere else?

"Whoever it was," I said, "would have had to be able to deactivate the alarm system. Unless she did. Bryant says it's tamper-proof."

"Nearly everyone here can do it; the family, all the key employees, and it's easy enough," Cloudsmith declared. "The man who installed the system is one of my principal advertisers, and he says there are two main switches, one in the house and the other at the foot of the stairs to the office. Both are turned off and on using the same transmitter you use to open the gates. The chapel here isn't on the system. Birds and rats could set it off. Ditto for the loggia and courtyard."

"Well," I said, "that lets me out, at least. Elissa didn't give me a transmitter until yesterday."

"Sorry," Cloudsmith said. "Alice Brooks reports hers missing since the morning after your arrival. Neither she nor the police have been able to find it anywhere."

"Meaning I could have stolen it?"

Cloudsmith nodded. "Bognor theorizes that you could have taken it from her handbag when you visited the office, then that night gone up to the winery when everyone thought you were in your room, and shut the alarm off. It's easy to do, you just point the thing."

"I see," I said, and managed a hollow laugh. "And my motive?"

Cloudsmith chuckled. "Our worthy policeman admits defeat there. For the moment, at least. Just as he's had to with everyone else who has a transmitter. Virtually every person has an ironclad alibi, and almost all the employees had a record of intense loyalty first to old Simon Seldridge and now to John and Bryant."

"Are you sure the alarm wasn't out of order?" I asked.

Cloudsmith shook his head. "That was one of the first things the police checked."

Cloudsmith put away his notebook and I told him then about Hester's inviting herself for dinner, her insistence that John accept her brewery chairman's offer, and her threat, if he didn't, to force him to by suing to break old Simon's will.

He shook his head. "Enough right there to make Elissa a prime suspect, I would have thought. And John."

"Possibly," I agreed. "Certainly they couldn't afford to have her sue them. But if either of them killed her would they have done it in such a self-destructive way? If they hadn't been able to buy more Merlot," I went on, "the Abbaye would be ruined and they'd have to sell out for less probably than Hester was offering."

"True," Cloudsmith agreed. "But are we forgetting passion? A fit of blind rage, perhaps. Or even a sudden cold decision to stop Hester right then and there?"

I'd thought of that, of the explosiveness in John and the deadly quality in Elissa's eyes during their bitter row with Hester. Elissa's apparent shock the next morning after seeing Hester's remains could have been, I realized, the acting performance of her life. And John's odd detachment, if he'd killed Hester, either simply a refusal to face the horror of what he'd done, or lack of guilt about it.

"No," I said. "That's always a possibility."

Except I thought, where did that leave me with my gut feeling that there was a definite connection between Hester's murder and the murder of Julio Garcia-Sanchez? Didn't an impulse killing perhaps rule out such a connection?

On that inconclusive note, and, frustratingly, with more unanswered questions than when we met, the eccentric old editor and I parted. He went out a small door across the chapel from the vestry which I saw opened on to a dirt parking area entered from the road running past the property. He held up a key. "Found this lying about a couple of years back," he said cheerfully. "Had a copy made, figuring it might be useful one day. You can never tell, can you?"

He waved, the little door creaked shut behind him. After he'd gone, I sat a while in the gloom and silence, thinking. I felt as though I were walking through a pit of snakes, for it had slowly crossed my mind that Cloudsmith himself could be suspect. What better way, if he were the guilty one, to preempt whatever investigating I might do than to join me in a partnership which would enable him to lead me away from any trail he'd possibly left?

Could he be a murderer, this cherubic little man? If he had a key to the chapel, could he not also through some connection have got himself a transmitter to shut off the alarm system and open the front gates? I wondered if Bognor had checked to see if anyone among the employees besides Alice Brooks had ever lost one at some time or another.

Working journalists are seldom wealthy, but Cloudsmith knew his way around the world of wine like a fox. Might he not have seen a last chance in life for the kind of luxurious living he'd always envied in others? Could he be the "front man" for Jaconello?

I found I had to agree with the detestable Bognor. Where brutal murder has been done, no one is free from suspicion.

11

I WAS UNCOMFORTABLE at a candlelit dinner that night with
John, Elissa, and Lureen. It is hard to enjoy the hospitality
of someone you'd just considered as possibly being guilty of
the most horrendous murder. I took refuge in trying to forge
ahead mentally with my sleuthing.

While many murderers had successfully covered their par-
ticipation in a crime, few I'd heard of had ever been able to
hide their reason for it, and I decided motive was what I
needed to uncover. For the moment, I could accept Julio
Garcia-Sanchez as most likely having been murdered because he could identify the saboteur. Hester, however, now
was a different question. Her just chancing to run into the
saboteur when on her way to a rendezvous with someone
else was too much of a coincidence for me to accept. For the
moment, also putting aside suspicion of John or Elissa, I had
to agree with Bognor that she'd probably been killed by the
person she'd gone to meet.

Somewhere between the main course of a delicious pheas-
ant en Daubiere and a delightful lemon souffle à l'Armagnac
dessert, and after several glasses of L'Abbaye de Ste. Denise
Chardonnay, vintage 1983, I decided I would not be likely

to find any motive here in the house. If her murderer was not someone in the family who couldn't stand her hated existence one minute longer, then there had to be a reason that was connected somehow with her brewery lover's offer and with what the Abbaye was all about—which was wine. Since wine was not dealt with down at the house but up at the winery, the most likely place to unearth anything there would be the offices—and by the time dinner was over, I'd determined that once the house was asleep, I'd go and have a look around.

From the moment I made up my mind, the evening dragged interminably. At about ten o'clock John and Elissa decided to call it a day. I stayed a while longer in the living room with Lureen, watching television, and finally went upstairs myself to wait out the rest of the evening. From my room, I could vaguely hear the television still on. Once I heard Lureen go out onto the terrace, and looking down from my window, I could see the glow of her cigarette.

About an hour later, I heard her come up to her room. She closed her door and then, softly, I heard the sound of her stereo.

For another hour I determinedly fought off waves of sleepiness and an overwhelming desire to go to bed. Finally, however, the stereo stopped and the house was silent. I decided it was then or never. Rousing myself, I left on my mission, dressed for the occasion in my running shoes and the dark green zip-up overalls I use for ballooning and which I thought would make good camouflage.

I knew Bognor had posted a police guard at the winery but I had to presume the winery alarm system had not been turned off because of it. I'd brought along my little pocket transmitter and downstairs my first stop was the library. I'd been in the hall the evening before when John went in, transmitter in hand, then came right back out. Remembering Cloudsmith telling me there were two master alarm switches, one at the foot of the office stairs, the other in the house, I decided John must have been turning the system on. I closed the library door quietly behind me, turned on a light, and found the alarm almost at once in a wall cabinet behind the door itself. I pointed my transmitter at a little round grill in its flat metal surface which I guessed was a receiving cell and pressed my transmitter button. There was a click and a red light just below it went out.

Certain I'd successfully silenced it, my next stop was the telephone alcove by the living room door. There was a large key rack there with several rows of keys, each with an identifying tag. I got out a pencil flashlight I always keep in my flight suit and easily picked out a shiny brass Yale key with a tag which said "Office." Taking it, I stole back across the hall and, as silently as possible, let myself out the front door.

There was a big golden moon hanging over the Mayacamas Mountains to the southwest; a harvest moon, I thought, hoping it boded well. Its pale light, however, could betray me and I took pains, crossing the front lawn, to keep to the deep shadows afforded by the eucalyptus and olive trees. One officer on duty lounged by a police cruiser parked at the entrance to the cloister; another sat on a tilted-back chair under the archway itself. They were chatting and smoking and the light from the cruiser's open door made them easily visible. I could but hope they were the only police there.

I stayed off the gravel drive which might be noisy under foot until I had to. Then, keeping a careful eye on the law, who fortunately had their backs turned, I came out of the protection of shadows and got across the gravel drive with a minimum of crunching sound.

My immediate objective was a narrow dirt path approaching the building from its vineyard side, and a rarely used back door into the bottling room. On my tour with Bryant, we had come down through the vineyards and gained access to the cloister that way.

I made it to the path and edged carefully along it, twice tripping over the gnarled trunks of vines which here and there grew right out of it. Not far away, perhaps only a hundred yards, the utility building loomed up out of the

surrounding vines, a great dark presence. This worried me
a little because I knew Roland Grunnigen had an apartment
there. Twice I thought I heard the voices of some of the
pickers who were quartered on the ground floor. At the
thought that in the dark I might bump into someone, I began
to feel a cold chill of fear. In my imagination that someone
could only be the murderer, and I very nearly gave it all up.

I finally reached the door and to my relief, I'd remembered
correctly—that it had no lock, only a latch. The door itself,
however, gave me a bad time. With little or no repair for
many years, it had sagged severely. It opened inward and its
bottom edge dragged and scraped noisily an inch at a time
over the stone floor no matter how hard I tried to prevent
it. I suppose the sound was actually not that much but to
me it was as though the building were coming down. Twice
I stopped, holding my breath, convinced the officers were
already halfway there to investigate. But nobody came and
when I'd pushed the door open a foot, I carefully squeezed
through.

Inside, I stopped and stared into the inky darkness. And
just as I did, saw a little red light wink on fairly high up to
my left. I moved an arm. Another light came on further
away to my right. Alarm sensors. I knew they continued to
work even when an alarm was turned off and held my
breath. Silence. No bells. No sirens. But how about the direct
line which sent a signal of intrusion to whatever police mon-
itored the alarm? I waited. If I'd made a mistake and hadn't
turned the system off as I was certain I had, surely the two
men on duty would be alerted at once by radio. A minute
went by. Perhaps two. I inwardly heaved a sigh of relief and
stepped forward.

I was very wary of flicking on my little pencil flashlight
but I could hardly risk stumbling about among cases of bottles, or inadvertently knocking bottles off a long conveyor
belt which I remembered lay between me and the other side
of the room. I kept the light low and made it safely past the
belt, almost ran into a stack of cases filled with empties, and

then took a chance and without the light reached the door of the loggia.

It opened easily and my prayer that I'd find nobody on the other side was answered. The loggia was pitch-dark but the cloister beyond, which was bathed in moonlight, seemed empty of any menace. In its center, the little fountain whispered faintly and, looking back at the archway entrance, I could see the glow of the officers' cigarettes, the two men themselves silhouetted by the interior light of the parked cruiser. I could also hear the occasional crackle of the cruiser's radio.

Certain they couldn't see me, I felt my way up the loggia, one outstretched hand groping for the door to the main office stairs. I tried to be dead silent, in fact could only hear the heavy pounding of my own heart. I think if my hand had contacted another hand or any part of a human body, especially a face, I would have been too terrified to scream. But my hand came in contact with nothing except, finally, the door's smooth varnished surface.

Opening it quietly, I slipped back into the building and into the small hall at the foot of the stairs. I felt around, found a light switch, then decided against it. There were no windows but if one of Bognor's men were to come down the loggia on a routine check, he might spot light from under the door itself. Upstairs, a second door to the office was locked, just as I expected it to be, but the key I'd taken fitted and I let myself in, then closed and locked the door again behind me.

I had determined to search John's office first. Using my flashlight, I crossed the reception room to it and went in. His windows looked out over the vineyards and were visible from the utility building but not from the house. I decided to take a chance, pulled his curtains, shut his door, and turned on the lights. Then, I methodically went through everything; his desk drawers, file case, bookcase, a table stacked with documents. A small safe defied me and I could only hope whatever was in it was unimportant.

Twenty minutes later, I turned off his lights and went to the main secretarial office with two documents I thought I should have. One was John's father's will, the other John's divorce decree from Hester with an attached court order setting out the division of marital property. From Bryant and Elissa I had a pretty clear idea of what both would contain, but either, I told myself, might have left out information which could be vital, or even lied to me, something I didn't like to think possible, especially where Bryant was concerned.

There was a copier in the office and when I'd copied both documents I put the originals back where I'd found them and shoved the folded copies deep into the leg pocket of my flight suit.

Hester's office, taken over by Bognor, was locked. I went into Bryant's. At first I found nothing. The desk drawers yielded only pens, pencils, and blank foolscap pads. Nor, at first, did the file case produce anything except various legal contracts having to do with equipment purchases and employees or product sales. Turning my attention to tax files in another drawer, however, I found the Abbaye's returns for a number of previous years. I took out the two for the current and past year and copied them.

When I'd put them back, I crossed the secretarial office to the room where I'd met Grunnigen and Alice Brooks. This turned out to be Grunnigen's office and it contained exactly what one would expect to find in the office of a man responsible for growing the grapes from which the estate wine was made. A mass of papers dealing with the details and complexity of following a grape from planted root to the crusher-stemmer emphasized the necessity for a viticulturist's constant presence at his vineyards, especially in the month before harvest. It made me wonder about notations I saw in Grunnigen's desk diary. In the previous six weeks or so, he had spent a considerable amount of time away from the Abbaye, mostly in San Francisco but twice going as far off as Santa Barbara.

I saw nothing else of particular interest. It was now well past 2:00 A.M. I was completely worn out from tension and I almost decided to skip Alice Brook's office next door until another time. A natural bent to thoroughness, I suppose, made me stick with it, although Alice seemed such an unimportant dynamic where the murder was concerned that I hardly expected to find anything.

I closed her door as I had those to the other offices and peered out her window. I could again just make out the dark outline of the utility building and I saw no lights in any of the windows. I pulled the drapes shut, turned on Alice's desk lamp, and set to work again.

There was nothing on the desk except a daily diary, some business letters, and memoranda obviously relating to the sales and marketing work she was doing. There was nothing of interest in her bookcase, either, nor on a worktable. A file drawer in her desk seemed to be entirely devoted to the family. There were folders for John and Elissa, for Bryant and Lureen and Hester, but glancing through them, it was at once obvious that their contents were purely biographical and solely for publicity purposes.

Her top desk drawer contained the usual writing material. In another drawer, there were only telephone directories. A bottom drawer was a repository for Alice's personal things; extra makeup, a hairbrush, and so on.

I started to close it when my eye was caught by the corner of a photo frame buried beneath the clutter. I lifted things away and looked. It was a five-by-seven glossy photo of Alice and Roland Grunnigen, taken on a beach and quite recently, I guessed, from the look of them. They were both in swimsuits and had their arms around each other, and Alice's head was resting lovingly against Grunnigen's shoulder.

I put the photo back and began to think. Framed photos usually weren't hidden in a bottom desk drawer. Why had this one been condemned to such obscurity? A clandestine romance, on display only when John or Bryant weren't about? That hardly seemed the answer. If you think the boss will mind, take the photo home.

I closed the drawer and started to leave the room when I had an afterthought which I very nearly didn't act on. I'd looked at Grunnigen's diary, why not Alice's, too? I went back to the desk and skimmed through the pages. Nothing seemed of importance at first; the pages were filled with appointments to meet various newspaper and magazine editors, to attend meetings of one sort or another, or to discuss a brochure with a printing firm.

I suddenly realized, however, that a number of entries went back several months and indicated meetings with someone in San Francisco noted only as M.T. I found the use of initials curious because with all other appointments she'd identified the person to meet by his or her full name.

I took the diary into the main office and copied those pages, about half a dozen of them, added the copies to the will, divorce decree, and tax returns I'd stuffed into my flight suit, and returned the diary to Alice's desk.

Then it happened.

I had just turned out her lights and gone on to the reception room when I heard a key in the lock of the office door. The unexpected sound caught me completely off-guard and I simply froze in terror.

Then the door opened all the way and the person came into the room from the darkness beyond. I found myself looking at none other than Alice Brooks herself.

12

EVERYONE HAS TIMES when they feel the biggest fool ever. Alice looked at me and I looked at Alice and, totally flustered, I blurted out the only excuse I could think of at the moment.

"Oh," I said, "you gave me such a fright. God knows who I thought was coming in. I've lost one of my earrings and couldn't sleep because of it—they were a gift from my late husband. I was here this evening with Elissa for a few minutes and I thought I might have dropped it someplace. I was almost certain I still had both of them when I went up to my room, but . . ."

At well past two in the morning it was so patently a lie and my weak smile so ineffective, I couldn't go on, and I compounded the ridiculousness of it by getting down on my hands and knees and pretending to look under the reception room couch. "No," I managed. "Not under there, either."

Alice still had not uttered a word. Nor moved. She simply stood in the doorway and stared. I rose to my feet again and stared back. The best defense is a strong offense.

She finally found her voice. "How on earth did you get in, Mrs. Barlow? I saw the alarm was off when I came upstairs but I'm surprised the police didn't stop you."

I managed a shrug. "They seemed busy in their car," I said "I just walked right by them and I have a key. How about you?"

For just an instant, she looked taken back at my question, then laughed. "I came through the chapel. Those of us who don't live here often do." And I remembered Cloudsmith's exit through the small door to what he told me was the employees' parking lot.

I began to gain confidence. Alice hadn't screamed or called out for the police, nor menaced me in any way. I was a guest of her employer and she was stuck with that and the remote chance, also, that I might be eccentric enough to be telling the truth. If she was playing a more sinister role than I immediately thought, I doubted I was in danger from her at this point. She would not cover up a previous murder by committing a second one unnecessarily. Besides that, unless she was armed, I thought I'd be more than a match for her.

She rose to the occasion and made a pretense of starting to look around for the missing earring. "How dreadfully upsetting for you, Mrs. Barlow. I'm so sorry. Did you sit on the couch here at any time?"

She made the gesture of lifting up the couch cushions and feeling behind them. I had to secretly admire her aplomb and told her I'd scoured every inch of the room and lifted up the cushions myself. It was at that point that she explained her own presence there at that hour.

"I have an appointment in San Francisco tomorrow morning," she said, "and I left some of the material I'll need here. I was at dinner up the valley when I remembered."

It wasn't true, of course; there were no San Francisco appointments scheduled in her diary for the morning. Or for the afternoon. But she'd done a far better job than I at lying, and I pretended to believe her. We both declared a silent truce after that and continued our desultory search until she had enough.

"I'll leave a note for the cleaning staff," she said "They're absolutely honest, Mrs. Barlow. If they find it, they'll turn it in.''

I thanked her and after one or two pleasantries, said good night and fled with the feeling that if ever two women had managed to cope with an impossibly embarrassing situation, it had been us. And wondering, too, what the real reason might be for her coming by at such an hour. Could she possibly be the person whom Hester claimed she had pressuring the Seldridges and whom Hester had the meeting with? Somehow I didn't think so. Nor, as I'd talked to Alice, had I been able to cast her further as a possible murderer. The role just didn't suit her.

My way out of the Abbaye was the same as my way in; down the pitch-dark loggia, feeling for the door to the bottling room which I navigated without a disaster, and then back along the narrow little path sandwiched between the vineyard and the building's outside wall. When I crossed the driveway, Bognor's two officers were still lounging in the archway, killing the dead hours of the night, the cruiser radio still cracking police business.

The house was silent. I returned the office key to the rack in the telephone alcove and made my way up to my room as quickly and quietly as possible. I certainly didn't want to get caught at this late stage. I was most worried about Lureen who I thought might be up again and wandering about. But neither she nor anyone else appeared, and, absolutely exhausted, I fell asleep almost the moment I got into bed.

I awoke to a midmorning California fog. A white mist covered the vineyards so I couldn't see much beyond the terrace when I looked out my window. It was nearly ten o'clock. Wondering what the day would bring, I showered and dressed casually and, pulling a cardigan over my shoulders against the morning chill, went down to the dining room for breakfast. José told me that Bognor was still very much at the winery and would descend after lunch with his forensic team for a thorough inspection of the house, including everyone's personal quarters and clothes. John was supervising the crushing of the morning's pick of Cabernet Sauvignon and Elissa had gone off early with Roland Grunnigen to see the man who was supplying the Merlot.

I declined any thought of watching the crushing operation and went back to my room, first to read the will and divorce papers. It seemed almost a futile effort. Both documents appeared straightforward enough and said exactly what Elissa and Bryant had told me. Seldridge left his two sons equal shares in the Abbaye, its land, vineyards, and winery, with John having the right to live in the principal residence in return for running the estate operation. No part of the Abbaye could be sold on its own, and neither brother nor his heirs could sell without the permission of the other or unless corporate liabilities exceeded assets. Further, each was bound to leave their share on their death to their legal issue. That brought me to John's divorce decree. The California court, under the state's property division laws, had granted Hester half of John's shares in the Abbaye providing that she, in her will, respected the dictates of Seldridge's testament, which she clearly had.

Next, I took out the tax returns. Again, I didn't learn much other than what I'd already surmised or picked up here and there from Elissa and Bryant. The returns showed precisely what sort of trouble the Abbaye was in. Both years reflected very large losses although the company's assets still far outweighed its liabilities. I found myself thoroughly awed, however, by what the winery and the property were worth. Their value was big money by any standard.

I put the returns away, and turned my attention to the pages of Alice's desk diary and the mysterious M.T. I ruled out a boyfriend for the framed photo I'd seen indicated that until recently, at least, her boyfriend had been Grunnigen. I probably would have given up on the initials if I had not found an entry which read: "Send budget and map." It was on a page where there was a lunch date with M.T. noted. I felt the two might be connected.

That speculation raised all sorts of questions. What

budget? Hers? The Abbaye's? If her own, why the map? And a map of what? My suspicions were immediately aroused. Could Alice be in with Jaconello or with some other unknown person also trying to get the Abbaye? I thought seriously of her. There was a touch of real hardness there and she was a woman who was passing the age when she could hope to find the luxury life I suspected she yearned for through a rich husband or a quantum leap in her career. Yes, she could well be fronting for someone, I decided, if there was enough money in it for her. I could also see her as an "insider" keeping the saboteur informed of the latest in the Seldridge's decline in fortune and, at the right time, letting him in to do the dirty work. She was familiar enough with the winery to move about it freely, even in the dark; she had a transmitter with which to shut off the alarm system. And she'd proved to me, at least, that she had a cool head in a tight spot.

The morning fled. I heeded José's luncheon bell and was having lunch on the terrace by myself when Roland Grunnigen went past on his way up through the hillside vineyards.

"John's looking for Alice. Have you seen her?"

I told him I hadn't and learned she apparently had not appeared for work. Could Alice actually have been telling the truth, I wondered, when she'd said she had a meeting in San Francisco?

"I think I heard her say something about a meeting in San Francisco," I said.

Grunnigen didn't think that likely.

There were important matters for her to take care of in the office, he said, and I could hardly tell him I thought her absence could be explained by a very late night. If she hadn't stayed at the Abbaye, she would not have made it to bed in Napa where she lived until at least a full hour after I did.

"Have you called her home?" I asked.

"Twice," he said. "No answer."

Grunnigen continued on his way, leaving me to wonder

what on earth Alice saw in him and again why their photo had been relegated to her bottom drawer. I also found myself wondering about his French accent. He made all the mistakes in English that most Frenchmen do who don't speak it perfectly, but just the same something about it didn't ring quite true to me.

I finished lunch, went to the telephone alcove, and made two calls. One was to New York and Joanna. Hester's murder hadn't been picked up by television or any New York papers and I certainly didn't want to risk a storm of unwanted daughter protection by telling her what had happened. Sounding her usual harried self, she accepted my canceling lunch and saying I was having such a lovely time that I planned to extend my stay a few days.

"Stay out of trouble, Mom."

"I'll let you know as soon as I get back," I promised.

The second call was to the head office of the West Coast brewery whose chairman had been Hester's lover and fiancé.

I asked for his secretary and when she came on the line, I told her I was editor of *Retirement* magazine. "We're doing a story on leading corporate executives who are soon calling it a day," I explained, and tried to sound as guileless as possible. "Would you happen to know if your boss has made plans to retire?"

There was no hesitation in her answer. He was going to step down in three months, she said. She also told me a lot of other things I didn't really want to know: he and his wife would be moving to Arizona; nothing would ever be the same without him; the board hadn't yet found a worthy successor. I wondered if she'd known about him and Hester.

When I'd finished the call, one thought was uppermost in my mind. Three more months and he would not have been able to order the Abbaye to be bought. Because of it, had she leaned too hard on the person she claimed was helping her sway the Seldridges? Could she even have been blackmailing them? Unless they were getting a big payoff, it was hard to see any of the Abbaye's loyal employees betraying them for any other reason.

I had hardly put the phone down when it began to ring. I hesitated, then picked it up and said it was the Seldridge residence.

A woman's voice asked me if John was there and when I said he must be at the winery office, she said she'd called there but nobody had answered.

That surprised me. Where were the secretaries? I glanced at my watch. It was past two o'clock. They all should have been back from lunch.

"Then is Mrs. Seldridge there?"

"I'm afraid not. She's in Sonoma for the day, I believe."

"Oh."

"May I help in any way? I'm a family friend," I said, stretching the truth a bit.

"Well, maybe." Hesitation, then, "If you could perhaps give John a message?"

"Of course."

"I share a house with Alice Brooks and I'm frightfully worried about her. She never came home last night. She wasn't here today either because the cat hadn't been fed when I came in and our telephone message machine was still on."

I said I'd find John immediately and let him know that she'd called and that I was sure Alice was all right. "She might have spent the night here," I said in an attempt to reassure.

But it was reassurance I didn't feel. My heart sank with a premonition that something awful had happened again.

I headed immediately for the winery and my worst fears began to be realized when halfway there, I saw an ambulance coming through the front gates and turning into the cloister.

I almost ran then. As I came into the cloister itself, there was a cluster of men at the open doors to the cuvier. Bognor was among them. I didn't get further. I was stopped by one of his officers. Before I could ask him what happened, John detached himself from the group and came my way.

"Margaret, is Elissa back?"

"I don't believe so."

His face was like stone. "It's Alice," he said. "She was found floating in the largest of the Cabernet vats."

13

SUDDENLY, THERE WAS MOVEMENT at the cuvier door as the ambulance men brought Alice out on a stretcher. They carried her across the cloister and right past where we were standing. They hadn't wasted time with a body bag, or even bothered to cover her with a sheet. They'd just dumped her on her back on the stretcher and the wine dripped from her sodden body, leaving a long line of pale red on the cloister's ancient paving blocks.

I didn't think I could bear to look at her; certainly I had no intention of doing so. But I did. One is drawn automatically to horror and death, even if only for the briefest glimpse. What I saw will remain with me forever: a bloated caricature of a woman, features contorted with the agony of not finding air to breath and finally drowning as the fermentation vat filled with juice from the wine press. Her flesh and skin, even her bulging eyes which now stared at nothing, were purple with the juice, as purple as the rag stuffed in her mouth and held in place with vineyard twine knotted so vise-tight that her lower jaw had been pulled down unnaturally, giving her the appearance of a hideous death's head.

She had been clubbed helpless first, I was to learn later, then bound and gagged before being shoved quite conscious through the empty fermentation vat's trapdoor, there to struggle and moan knowing quite well what her fate would be come morning when the vat was pumped full. In a way, I found her death as horrifying, if not more so, than Hester's. It seemed to me more calculated and thus, if possible, more vindictive.

I glanced at John. Staring at her body as she went by, his expression was first one of shocked horror, then suddenly as some thought struck him, I thought one of naked fear.

As she was put in the ambulance, Bognor approached us. "We had a call this morning, Mrs. Barlow," he said in his flat colorless tone. "Someone said you were seen leaving the winery around two-thirty A.M. I'll expect your visit to my office upstairs . . ." The horrid little man paused to glance at his watch, ". . . say in an hour? That will give you the opportunity to think how to explain to me what you were doing. Meanwhile you will remain away from your room while my forensic people have a look around."

I could find nothing to say, and with what could only be described as a smile of gloating pleasure, he beckoned John to follow him and headed for the office.

Who on earth had seen me? I wondered, then, standing there in the bright sunlight, I suddenly felt the back of my neck prickle, for the obvious had finally occurred to me. Surely it would have been the murderer himself who telephoned the police. Who else? Perhaps the whole time I had been in the winery, almost certainly when I left, he had also been there, possibly at times only a few feet away and watching my progress.

I wandered aimlessly until it was time to meet with Bognor. Uppermost in my mind was that except for her murderer I was the last person who had seen Alice alive. And I, the last person she had seen. The thought gave me a deeply disturbing sense of intimacy with her death.

One is never fully prepared for the nastiness of someone

like Bognor and I was no exception. I had a bad hour of it.
A second particularly brutal murder had not only occurred
but had occurred right under his nose. His mood was as vile
as anyone could imagine, and I found myself thinking of the
two officers on guard whom I'd so carefully avoided and
wondering what their fate was to be.

His questioning was relentlessly repetitive. Why had I left
the house at that hour? Had I planned to meet Alice? How
long had I known Alice? And what he thought would be a
catch question: What weapon had I used to cudgel her into
submission? Where was it? He ignored the fact that had I
been the murderer, I would hardly have answered that one.

I admitted to leaving the house. But I denied seeing Alice,
deciding to take a chance on there not having been a second
anonymous phone call. I also admitted to copying Seldridge's will, the divorce papers, tax returns, and some pages
from Alice's diary. It was just as well I did because I hardly
had when one of his men brought them in. The forensic
people had recovered them from my room.

The copying really got to Bognor. One glance and every
suspicious bell in his being must have clanged mercilessly.
He waved some of the copies. "And just what is all this for?"

I decided I might as well tell him the truth. He might not
believe it but he wasn't going to believe anything else, either.
"To help me find Hester's murderer," I said.

"To help you find a murderer . . ." he repeated. "To help
you . . ." He steamed, unable to speak further, then finally
got out a choked, "The police are here for that, *Mrs.* Barlow."
He had a way of emphasizing the Mrs. as though my married
title were somehow a front for some unsavory activity.

"You can't blame me for trying," I countered. "I want to
go home."

"Do you really?" He then began again with his questions.
Why had I made copies? What did I expect to get out of
them? How much progress had I made in finding the murderer? What did I expect to do when and if I did find him
or her?

Eventually he wound down and let me go. Back at the house, I spent an hour putting away things in my room which the forensic people had gone through. Ransacked might be a better word. But although Bognor had confiscated my night's work, I had no problem remembering most of it, and I decided my next step would be to review it with Cloudsmith, regardless of any vague suspicions where he was concerned. I went downstairs to the now familiar telephone alcove, arranged to meet him at his newspaper in Napa, and after writing a quick note to Elissa, who had not returned yet, went out and started up my rented car. The front gates were guarded by a uniformed officer. I held my breath. Would he stop me? Almost to my surprise, he didn't and with a sense of relief difficult to describe at just getting away for even a short time, I drove away from the Abbaye.

THE VALLEY RECORDER was located thirty miles to the south at the beginning of the Napa Valley and on the outskirts of Napa City. It was in an old, worse-for-wear red brick Victorian warehouse, entirely in keeping with Cloudsmith's eccentric character.

A concession to modern times in the form of an oversized electric sign on the roof told me I was at the right newspaper even before I pulled off the potholed macadam back street and parked close by under an immense and shading sycamore tree.

The newspaper's office occupied the front of the building. It consisted of a single large room graced by two bedraggled potted palms, several slow-turning fly-specked ceiling fans, and four littered wooden desks which had seen better days. At one sat a woman nearly as old as Cloudsmith and with the authoritative air of being the person who ran the place. She wore rimless pince-nez glasses on a nose I could only describe, even charitably, as a beak; her snow white hair was piled into a scraggly top knot; and a high lace collar topped a shapeless floral print dress which hung from her bony frame like a limp curtain.

At another desk which faced a moth-eaten, wall-mounted stuffed fish, a pale effeminate young man stared at a computer totally out of keeping with the antiquity of the other office furnishings. A reporter? I had the impression he had never seen a single ray of California's famous sunshine.

A partition of glass surrounded a corner cubicle. Gold lettering on its door, some of it worn away, announced this as the territory of the "Editor-in-Chief," thus separating Cloudsmith from his minions.

Beyond all this, I could see, and hear through another open door at the back of the room, the printing and folding presses which, along with the type-setting tables, translated daily news gatherings into a readable material that eventually ended up on people's breakfast tables.

The clatter from the presses when I entered was deafening and the whole place reeked of machine oil, printers' ink, and newsprint as only an old-fashioned country newspaper can. I had hardly announced myself to the secretary, who greeted me with frosty suspicion, when Cloudsmith, on his telephone, spotted me from where he sat at a rolltop desk as old as he and beckoned me to come into his sanctuary. He greeted me with an effusive welcome, apologizing for the noise and explaining that they were running off flyers for a traveling carnival. "Nowadays," he said, "we have to print anything we can to keep our heads above water. Television! People don't read anymore. Someday, the only place you'll see newspapers is in museums."

He had heard about Alice, of course—Bognor had told him—but only the barest details, and from me he wanted whatever information I could supply, jotting down everything I said in a reporter's notebook. As he did, there was again the steely-eyed air of professionalism about him.

Looking up over his desk at some framed newspaper front pages, I was impressed by the layout and the seriousness of the diverse headlines, to say nothing of the two framed state awards for editorial writing of outstanding merit. Glory without money? A condition that has driven many to des-

perate acts, I thought, and I began to wonder how much of
his put-on eccentricity, like Charwood's buffoonery, was an
act to lull people. The average person, I among them, is far
less likely to be suspicious of a clown.

After he'd virtually insisted I describe Alice's appearance
"in mortuus", as he said, and I had filled him in on my
session with Bognor, I recounted my nighttime sortie into
the office, and what I had done there. I did so not without
feeling uncomfortable. For all the while I kept thinking that
if my seeing Cloudsmith as a possible suspect, even though
vaguely, ever proved correct, he would have to be silently
laughing at me.

I detected nothing in his face or manner, however, which
would support this, and, eventually lulled away once more
from unpleasant thoughts about him, told him about being
caught in the act by Alice herself.

"If you report this to your friend Bognor," I said flatly,
"it's the end of our partnership."

"A journalist's perogative, as you know, dear lady, is to
protect his sources," he said by way of reply. "Don't worry
yourself."

"Bognor's confiscating all my copying isn't a disaster," I
told him. "I can pretty much remember everything that was
in the will and the divorce papers. There weren't any surprises except possibly in the diaries."

"Diaries?"

"Alice's and Grunnigen's. But mostly hers. A few of their
notations seemed to me a little odd. Hers was the only one
I copied."

"Odd in what way?"

"Well, Grunnigen's because he was away from the Abbaye
quite often this month and last when, because of the harvest
coming up, I thought it might have been important for him
to be keeping on eye on his vineyards."

Cloudsmith nodded slowly and said, "There could be
something there, yes. But not necessarily sinister. Perhaps
there was a special lady friend. That might explain the row

with Alice you said you believe you walked in on and the photo being committed to the obscurity of a bottom drawer. He has quite a reputation with the women, that young man. What about Alice's?"

"Dates she had with someone."

"Ah? Who?"

"That's just it. I don't know. She only refers to the person as M.T."

"M.T.?" The old man looked thoughtful again and then, to my surprise, straightened up sharply. "M.T.? You did say M.T.?"

"Yes."

"Well, I'll be," he said. "And you have no idea who that could be?"

"None at all."

"My guess is Marcel Turbo. I'll bet you anything. Here." He reached to the back of his rolltop to pluck a photo from a pile. "Turbo Wines. America's Choice and American Eagle Red. One hundred and eighty million gallons a year sold in supermarkets alone. That takes a lot of grapes and Turbo buys from everyone."

I looked at the photo, an aerial shot. It showed a vast complex, sprawling over several hundred acres, of warehouses, smaller buildings, and hundreds of giant fermentation vats.

"The vats are all outdoors," I said.

"Too many and too big to put under a roof," Cloudsmith explained. "Some of the big ones hold a million gallons each."

"But what about the sun?" I asked. "Don't they get awfully hot?"

He shook his head. "Their temperature is controlled by a cooling system and can be regulated to the half-degree depending on exactly what fermentation heat is required for a particular grape to get a particular taste. It appears," he added, "as though our Alice might have been trying to swing a little deal with Turbo."

"But why," I asked, "would a high-volume operation like Turbo want a comparatively little vineyard like the Abbaye?"

"Perhaps the same reason as Jaconello," Cloudsmith said. "To market a top-quality vintage wine, although his underlying purpose would be a little different. Putting out one or two superior wines, a top vintage Sauvignon or Chardonnay, say, would be good advertising and publicity for all his wines in general. What easier way to do that than to buy a vineyard and winery which already had a reputation for the very best?"

"But would he have to stoop to either sabotage or murder to do it?" I insisted. "He must have all kinds of money and influence and hardly needs to take that sort of risk."

"You're right," Cloudsmith admitted. "He doesn't have to. And I don't think he would. Marcel is one tough hombre—you'd have to be to get where he is—but I know him. He's not crazy and I can't see him being that devious, or dangerous." He shook his head sadly. "Poor Alice. She wasn't always the wisest woman when pursuing what she wanted. I can think of a number of editorial toes she stepped on, granting exclusives to more than one person. But she hardly deserved what happened to her. She spent many a night at the Abbaye office, I know, usually coping with some sort of whimsicality on John's part. She once told me he was perfect hell to work for. Dictatorial, arbitrary, demanding. Couldn't care less about her feelings or her time. More than likely she was in the office the night Hester was murdered and had the terrible luck to see who did it."

I didn't think so but decided for the moment to keep my thoughts to myself.

"I think I'll go see Turbo," I said, "and try to get an answer of some sort direct from the horse's mouth. You can never tell, can you? At least I'll find out if he actually *was* the M.T. Alice was seeing."

Cloudsmith looked doubtful. "Do you think he'll tell you?"

"Why not?" I asked. "If Turbo was taking advantage of

someone else's disaster, there was nothing illegal about that or even immoral. And from his point of view, buying out John before the banks closed in would, in fact, not only save John from all the problems of bankruptcy but make him a very rich man. If the man indeed had a deal with Alice, he might easily talk now that she's dead. So how about an introduction?''

To my surprise, Cloudsmith shook his head. "Afraid you're on your own there. Turbo isn't speaking to me.'' He pointed to one of the framed front pages on his wall. I saw an article at the bottom of the page headlined, "Marcel's Mega Merlot Monster.''

"I took him to task for reducing the standard of his already reduced rotgut in order to scoop up one more supermarket chain. In other words, how greedy can you get when you've already made more out of wine than any man in history? Marcel doesn't take kindly to criticism.''

"I'll give him a call myself, then,'' I said.

"And good luck getting through to him,'' Cloudsmith said. "He's divorced and surrounded by admiring office protectors of the female variety.''

"The more protectors, the more vain the person protected usually is,'' I said. "And I've never met a vain man who didn't like having his picture taken.''

15

IT WAS JUST as Cloudsmith had said. The protection was considerable and all female. It began on the telephone when I called him that afternoon the moment I got back to the Abbaye.

"Could you tell me what it's about, Miss Barlow?"

"*Mrs*. Barlow. Yes. I'm a photo-journalist. I'm doing an article on California wine makers for a New England newspaper and I want to include Mr. Turbo."

"Just a moment, please."

Silence. Then, another young female voice. "This is Mr. Turbo's secretary. How may I help you?"

"I'd like to make an appointment to see Mr. Turbo."

"Could you please tell me what this is in reference to, Miss . . . Miss . . ."

"Barlow. Margaret Barlow."

"Miss Barlow."

"*Mrs*. Barlow." And again I went through the wine story routine.

"I see. Well, if you'd like, I can send you our standard publicity package. It has photos and a biographical sketch. I think you'd find it very interesting."

"Thank you," I said, "but I don't work that way."

"He has meetings all day, I'm afraid. And then he's going away tomorrow for several weeks. Why not give me your number and I'll ask him to call you."

Sometimes, the best way to demolish a wall is with dynamite. I said sweetly, "Oh, please do." And gave the Abbaye de Ste. Denise house number. "Perhaps you wouldn't mind giving him a message in the meantime?" I added.

"Of course."

"Please tell Mr. Turbo that on a balloon flight last week I already photographed him at his swimming pool. They're terrific shots. I used a Mark IV aerial camera with a one-thousand-millimeter telescopic lens, and he and his young lady friend look as though I was standing only ten feet away. Tell him that given the nature of the pictures he might want to see them himself before I send them off to a magazine. He'll know what I mean."

Dead silence, then. "Mrs. Barlow? Hello? Hello?" I put the receiver down gently and waited. He might not have been swimming for the past six months, for all I knew, or even have a swimming pool. And the chances of my hitting on the right day of the year for him to be indecently romping about with a girlfriend were minimal. I didn't think, however, that it made any difference. If nothing else, curiosity would get the better of him.

I was right. It took five minutes. I let the phone ring a good half-dozen times before I picked it up. "Hello?"

"Mrs. Barlow, please." The voice was resonantly masculine.

"Speaking."

"Oh, hello, Mrs. Barlow. I'm Marcel Turbo. You were trying to reach me, I believe." And then followed apologies for the difficulty I'd had and could I drop by and see him in the morning?

"Say, eleven o'clock? Do you know where we are?"

"You seem to occupy most of central California," I said. He laughed and I took down some driving instructions and that was that. He made no mention whatsoever of my aerial photographs nor of his supposed extended trip. Neither did I.

Meanwhile, the Abbaye's winery operation was back to square one. The Health Department had ordered everything shut down pending inspection and the entire Cabernet Sauvignon crop was at risk as well as the newly acquired Merlot.

Bryant came up from San Francisco the moment he'd heard the news about Alice. He had a dozen encouraging ideas on how to refinance the whole Abbaye operation; how to fend off the banks; how to raise new money. He managed to get John out of a totally black mood during which he barely spoke to anyone, and Elissa, who was taking this new disaster far better than he, was obviously grateful to Bryant for it. I was, too—I'd had enough of cold surliness—and as I warmly returned Bryant's kiss on my cheek when we said good night, I realized I was beginning to find him quite attractive.

In the morning, I skipped breakfast and left for my date with Marcel Turbo before anyone else was up, and, to my relief, with my departure once again ignored by the officer on guard at the gates.

Where wine is concerned, California is divided roughly into nine separate districts ranging from Mendocino and the Lake Counties on the Pacific coast in the far northwest to the section south of Los Angeles. By far the largest of these districts, producing 70 percent of the state's wine, is the great San Joaquin or Central Valley, some seventy miles wide and stretching four hundred and eighty miles from just north of Los Angeles right up to the Napa Valley. Turbo Wines was located outside a little town named Crows Landing about an hour's drive from San Francisco's Bay area and close to the San Joaquin River.

Arriving late the following morning, I found it an even more staggering place than it looked in Cloudsmith's aerial photograph. A security officer at the heavily guarded main entrance gave me directions to the administration building, and before I knew it I reached the guest parking area in front of a sprawling two-story modern structure entirely surfaced in green glass.

A uniformed guard escorted me through a front lobby with fountains and shrubbery. An elevator with soft lights and piped-in music took me up the one flight. Getting out, I found myself in a plush reception area and was met at once by the first of the protection squad, a stunning-looking young blond receptionist. Security had unquestionably telephoned ahead my arrival. She took one look at my cameras and I was in.

"Mrs. Barlow?"

"Yes."

She gave me a smile to melt cold granite, pressed phone buttons, and announced my arrival with a reverence which was embarrassing. Almost at once, an even lovelier, if possible, young woman appeared; the exalted secretary.

I was again greeted like royalty. Doors flew open, carpeted corridors hung with important artwork blurred by, and in moments I was ushered into an ultra-modern office and the hallowed presence of Turbo himself.

Whatever my image of Turbo before this moment, the reality, as with Charwood, was hardly what I expected. He stood up from behind a vast uncluttered desk and said, "Hello, Margaret."

I stared a moment and then was unable to control my laughter, mostly at myself. Marcel Turbo was none other than the devastingly attractive man who had flirted with me at the cocktail party after my last day of ballooning.

16

HIS GRIN was a mile wide. "Compromising photos from a balloon? Margaret, shame on you. I knew who you were the moment my secretary gave me your name. You scared the hell out of her, though. She believed every word of it. Should I tell her the truth? That you forgot to put film in your camera?"

I shook my head, for once keeping my mouth shut. He insisted on champagne to celebrate our reacquaintance. I didn't object and the secretary, now as obsequious as she'd been hostile, brought in a bottle already well-chilled. It was a very expensive French vintage.

"Not mine, I'm afraid," he said. "So, tell me. What's this all about? If I remember correctly, you already have a respectable picture of me."

I explained and it took a while because I decided to trust him and so left nothing out. I told him how far I'd come in my thinking about all three murders and about previous murders I'd investigated. I told him about my strange partnership with Cloudsmith, and about Charwood and Jaconello's endless efforts to buy the Abbaye, and finally about Bognor grounding me.

He listened silently but attentively, and when I finished, he was thoughtful a moment, then shook his head. "I don't like the sound of this, Margaret. I know Bognor and he's a first-class bastard. You've got to have a lawyer."

"I have one," I said. "Bryant Seldridge volunteered."

"Bryant did? Well, you can't go wrong with him. What does he say?"

"He thinks it's probably not wise to formally confront Bognor with a lawyer right away. He thinks Bognor would see that as a challenge, particularly where I'm concerned."

Marcel nodded. "He's probably right. But it's safe to say only until Bognor gets wind of your trying to beat him to a murderer, which it's also certain he will sooner or later. The moment he does, I can guarantee he'll have you locked up on some excuse or other. Look, the intelligent thing for you to do is forget this whole mess. I have a helicopter out back. I can spirit you to a major airport outside of California in less than an hour and Elissa can send your things on by courier. Bryant has some political clout and so do I, and if Bognor is stupid enough to try to extradite you, we can probably stop him."

I thought of Julio Garcia-Sanchez and Hester and Alice. "Thank you," I said. "But I'll pass on that."

Marcel stared. "Margaret, you're crazy. Besides Bognor, you do understand, don't you, that you're dealing with a murderer who is unquestionably psychotic? Maybe the last person you'd ever suspect?"

"I know that. Perhaps even two of them. I'm not sure Garcia-Sanchez and then Hester and Alice were killed by the same person. The possible motives are so different."

Marcel shook his head slowly, giving me up as hopeless. "Besides crazy, you're also incorrigible."

He studied me a moment, surrendered and gave me up for lost, and favored me with the same incredible smile he had at the Napa cocktail party. "Okay," he said. "How about lunch?"

He did not wait for my answer. He shot orders into his

desk speaker and before I could even make a pretense of protestation, I found myself whisked away from the sanctity of his office to a helicopter all warmed up and waiting for us behind the building.

No pilot for this man. Just the two of us took off for the trip, first across the Central Valley with its mile upon mile of orchards, vegetable produce, and vineyards, then skimming the slate-colored waters of San Francisco Bay. I didn't talk the whole way. I just looked and loved every minute of it. When we landed near San Francisco's Fisherman's Wharf, we were met by a Rolls-Royce convertible with a liveried English chauffeur who drove us to a luxurious multi-star restaurant on Nob Hill. I waited to raise the real reason for my visit until Marcel had ordered more champagne, Russian caviar, and our entrees. Then, I finally said, "Now. Alice Brooks. 'Fess up."

"Why not?" he said. "The poor woman's dead, bless her." He took a breath. "Sure, we turned each other on once, but it was just play, a few weeks' worth, no romance, and that was that."

"How long ago?"

"Two years now. Maybe two and a half. Then we stopped seeing each other. I think I was just balm to an unhappy heart. She'd had an affair with John Seldridge and I think had marriage in mind when Elissa came along."

I remembered John's odd expression of fear as the ambulance men took Alice away. An affair with Alice would not have explained it. What else was there?

Marcel went on to tell me that out of the blue Alice had called him one day about six months ago and had come to see him. "She was involved with Roland Grunnigen," he said. "Well, perhaps more than just involved. She said she was in love. And with John in serious trouble, she wanted to try to buy him out and have Roland as the new L'Abbaye de Ste. Denise vintner. She didn't feel disloyal; she's never really forgiven John for Elissa. It was sad, too, because Alice was at least ten years older than Roland and I think setting him up in business was the way she hoped to keep him."

"What was her pitch to you?" I asked. "You'd get a high-grade wine for advertising?"

"Exactly," he replied. "And I almost went for it."

"But didn't. Why not?"

"Unforeseen events. Grunnigen suddenly dropped her. He found somebody else, apparently. I think Cloudsmith's right about that. Witness his diary, all those absences in town when he should have been at the Abbaye."

"But you didn't need a deal with Alice to buy out John," I said. "You must have had other reasons for calling it off."

I waited. His face, when he finally spoke, was sad. "You're right, Margaret. There were. Or one reason, anyway." He fiddled with his wineglass. "This will be hard to believe—most people wouldn't—but I hate this damned mass production business. Every single cheap jug worth. What I've always wanted to do is what John Seldridge is doing, live and work in a small vineyard and winery and produce estate wines which would compare favorably with any of the French greats. The real reason I turned Alice down is that I desperately want John Seldridge to succeed. He doesn't know it but I'm one of his biggest fans."

To say the least, I was surprised. But I also believed him. Marcel had spoken with utter sincerity and I asked him why on earth he didn't do what John was doing. Surely he had the resources.

"Of course," he answered. "But the time for me to do it was fifteen years ago, when I first started here. Now it's too late."

"Why?"

"Because when you build something as big as Turbo Wines, you also build major responsibilities that you can't just turn your back on. I have a huge work force dependent on me, hundreds of men along with their wives and children. Then there are my own children, alimony to the ex, investors who trust me to get results. The years go by. What made you do it all in the first place no longer interests you, and you always plan to do what you really want to do. Then one day you wake up and you realize you're trapped in a full-time job with no room for anything else and no escape."

I felt sad for him. I suddenly saw him with all his wealth and surrounded by all those sexy beautiful women as a very lonely person. But I couldn't change that for him, and his airing of his griefs wasn't going to help me with what I had to do. I got us back on to the Abbaye murders. "Let's talk about Jaconello," I said.

"Sure, what about him?"

"He tried very hard to buy the Abbaye. Elissa thinks it's just because John said no."

"Elissa is probably right. Jaconello is not a man who knows what the word no means. And he's also absolutely ruthless when it comes to getting what he wants. In his travels he once bought up a whole village in Peru then forcibly evicted everyone just so he could get the decorative village fountain they'd denied him." Marcel paused to look at me hard, then said. "You think he might be behind the sabotage, is that it?"

"He's as good a guess as any," I replied, "if what you tell me about him is true. And if he *is* behind it, then he's as responsible for the death of Garcia-Sanchez as the horror who did the actual killing."

"What about Hester?"

"I don't think she was murdered by the same person. And not even for the same reason unless, generally speaking, both murders were committed by persons who are out after the Abbaye. And I don't think whoever killed Garcia-Sanchez killed Alice, either."

"Who did? Hester's murderer?"

"Quite likely."

"But why?"

"Because of you," I said. I smiled when Marcel looked taken aback and explained. "I think Alice died because someone discovered she was double-dealing them with you and therefore saw her, also, as a threat. Can you think of anyone who might have known Alice was trying to line you up as a buyer?"

Marcel was thoughtful a moment. "Not specifically. Alice was very discreet. But once when she called me from the Abbaye we both suddenly realized somebody was listening in. We hung up promptly."

"But perhaps not promptly enough."

Marcel's eyes were disturbed. "And whoever it was then killed her. You could be right, I suppose. I wonder if we're talking about Jaconello again."

"Jaconello or somebody we don't know of yet, although Jaconello's name does keep cropping up, doesn't it? And so does Harry Charwood's as his possible front man. What about him?"

"Harry?" Marcel thought it over for a moment. "You called him a buffoon but I once saw a movie in which the circus murderer turned out to be the clown. Harry is forever broke so unless he's working for Jaconello or for someone else, one has to wonder where he planned to get the money to buy the Seldridges out."

Marcel stopped and looked at me sharply. "You know, we keep saying Seldridges. It wasn't always both Bryant and John. It started off just John."

I asked him to explain and he told me that only two weeks before Simon Seldridge died, he and the old patriarch had dined together after a wine-makers' convention in San Francisco. Seldridge had candidly worried about the future of the Abbaye and the arrangement he'd made for it in his will.

"He said Bryant was very well off from his law practice and had no real interest in wine so he'd made John the sole beneficiary," Marcel explained. "But he'd also tagged Hester as a first-class gold digger. If he were to die before a divorce, California law would give her half the company, he said. I suggested he change his will and include Bryant so the most she'd get would be a quarter share in the Abbaye, but he said no, Bryant might eventually want to sell out and he didn't want to worry that his two sons might someday be at each other's throats. I argued with him. Bryant and John are both reasonable men, albeit with different temperaments, but he was quite adamant about it and when Simon had his mind set, that was that."

Then what on earth had caused the old man to change his mind so abruptly?

Marcel had no explanation and, with a frustrating sense that there was an important element behind the murders I had seen or heard but, somehow missed, I was choppered back to Crows Landing and Turbo Wines where I reluctantly surrendered Marcel to his phalanx of protectors.

17

ON THE RETURN to the Napa Valley, I hardly noticed the scenery. Completely preoccupied, searching my mind for that missing element, I went over and over every single moment I could remember since I'd arrived at the Abbaye de Ste. Denise. I began right at the beginning with the conversation with Elissa in my room the first night and everything she'd said to me since. Recalling as much as possible telltale tones of voices and expressions as well as words, I went through everything Bryant and Cloudsmith had told me, too, and the questions Bognor had asked. And whatever Harry Charwood had said.

And thinking I might have missed some tiny clue somewhere in Hester's own words, I even concentrated on the night of her murder, trying as much as possible to recall every moment of her before-dinner arrogance as well as the after-dinner row in the living room.

I thought again of John's expression on seeing Alice. Could the fear in his eyes have been because he saw himself in serious danger from something he knew about her death and possibly Hester's, too?

Mentally, too, I finally reviewed all the papers I'd copied

and taken from the office the night of Alice's murder: the will, the divorce decree, the tax returns, and the diaries.

I got nowhere.

Traffic in the Bay area was rush-hour heavy and it was late before I finally reached the Abbaye. Driving through the big iron gates and past the archway entrance to the cloister, I noticed that the two officers on guard were not the same ones as from two nights ago. They weren't lounging and smoking, either. One at once stepped briskly into the driveway to stop me, and ordered me to identify myself before allowing me to continue on.

To my surprise, the house was dark when I reached it and there were no parked cars. I was jumpy with my thoughts and it gave me a shock when José unexpectedly opened the door just as I turned the handle to do so myself.

"Good evening, Mrs. Barlow."

"José. Where is everybody?"

"Mr. and Mrs. Seldridge called to say they were going to spend the night in San Francisco at Mr. Bryant's. Mrs. Seldridge left you a note on the hall table. Have you had dinner, madam?"

I told him I hadn't and he said he'd fix something at once and call me.

"Just a salad would be fine, José. I had a big lunch."

He nodded and started to turn away when I said, "Where is Miss Lureen?"

His smile evaporated. He hesitated, glancing up the stairs before he answered. "I believe she's in her room, madam."

With that, he went off quickly toward the kitchen. I picked up the bright blue envelope with my name on it and extracted Elissa's note. She apologized for leaving me on my own for dinner but said Bryant wanted both her and John to meet a possible financier. Bognor had been on the warpath all day, she said, and the Health Department had insisted on steam-sterilizing all the fermentation vats even though poor Alice could only have caused problems with one of them. They were going to have to write off yet another year's crop.

"We're spending the night in San Francisco, so don't wait up for us," she'd written. "And do ask José for anything you might want."

I pocketed the note and went upstairs. Halfway there, I heard what I thought were low voices in the corridor and when I'd reached the landing I realized what I'd heard was someone moaning. I think I knew what the sound meant before I reached Lureen's open door, but my mind refused to recognize it.

I stopped when I got there. I'm afraid I couldn't help it. Stopped and for a moment, until I came to my senses, just stared. What I saw was Lureen and Roland Grunnigen on her bed, naked and making love. When I finally moved, and it seemed an eternity, although I'm sure I didn't stand there more than three seconds, I did so as quickly and as silently as I could. But Grunnigen happened to turn his head and see me. He froze an instant in his rhythm, then, with a faint smile, went right on as though I didn't exist.

Twenty minutes later, when José rang the dinner gong, I hardly dared come out of my room. Lureen's door was closed now and I could hear the shower hissing.

After a light dinner, I went out onto the terrace. Standing in the relative coolness of the night air, perfumed by the scent of the vineyard's grapes, I suddenly had an idea. Could I perhaps not reproduce the strange scraping sound I had heard the night of Hester's murder and at least clear up *that* mystery?

I moved a metal chair. Its legs screeched on the flagstones. No, that wasn't it. I tried a wooden chaise lounge. No luck there, either, in the wood's shuddering chatter. Emboldened, I went to the pool and moved first a heavy flower pot, then Lureen's sun stretcher. It was neither of those.

I was facing the pool, my back to the house. I straightened, wondering what to move next. And turned.

My heart stopped. There was someone standing right behind me.

I didn't scream, although I did gasp quite loudly. Then I

saw it was Lureen. "Good heavens," I said, "you gave me the most awful fright."

She didn't reply to that. Instead, she said, rather stiffly, "Mrs. Barlow, could I have a word with you, please?"

"Of course. Shall we go back inside?"

Without speaking, she returned to the living room. I followed. After we sat down a distance apart on the couch, she stared at me with the oddest expression, then rose abruptly and found a cigarette in a case on a table and lit it. I watched in silence. She seemed terribly nervous, almost explosively so. When she sat down again, she poured some wine into a glass, drank it, and then, without looking at me, just staring down into the empty glass, said abruptly, "You saw us, didn't you? Roland said you stood and watched."

"Not exactly."

"But you saw."

"Yes, I'm sorry. I couldn't help it. Your door was wide open. There's nothing to be ashamed of. You're not a child and sex is okay. And, after all, it's not something I wouldn't know about."

"It's not what you think," she said. "It's not just sex. I can find that in any bar in Napa or Sonoma, all I want and anytime I want it. Christ, they line up."

"I'm sure."

Suddenly, to my astonishment, I saw she was crying.

"Lureen," I prodded gently.

"We're in love," she whispered. "Crazy in love. We can't help it. Can you understand?"

"Of course."

"I love him and he loves me. I mean, really. And if John or Bryant finds out it could be awful. That would be it. They'd fire Roland."

"But why?"

"Don't you see? They'd be convinced he was just after the money. Maybe even the Abbaye. And he isn't. Honestly. We can't help being in love. It just happened."

"What about Alice?"

For an instant her eyes hardened. "What about her?"

"Did she know? About you and Roland?"

"Roland told her."

"And?"

"Well, okay, I felt a little sorry for her, sure. But she had her chance. She was suffocating him. And she was getting old."

She had another drink. Her hand was shaking and I said, "Look, Lureen, there's no need to be upset. You're worried I'll tell, is that it?"

She raised a tear-stained face and nodded, and I felt sympathy for her for the first time. Her life to date, in spite of money, or perhaps because of it, had hardly been an emotional gravy train.

"Well, don't worry," I said firmly. "You're not a child and there's nothing wrong with being in love. Anyway, what you do is your business. I certainly wouldn't even consider telling, although I think you're a little silly to be so anxious about their reaction."

"You don't know John." Anger suddenly crept into her voice.

"Perhaps not as well as you, no."

"He'd go crazy if I was ten minutes late coming home from a high school dance. And he had to vet every boy I went out with. Jealous. He always wanted me all for himself."

My immediate reaction was to consider what John's side of the coin must have been. Lureen had to have been the original teenage handful. I thought of Hester, her selfishness and self-indulgence, and John's lonely job of raising a child who wasn't his. I had no answer. The best I could come up with was a stale platitude. "I'm sure he only had your best interests at heart."

She'd clearly heard that one before. She shot me a knowing and dismissive look and drew on her cigarette, watching the smoke curl. Then suddenly she rose and, with a murmured good night and a faint smile, was gone.

Now what, I asked myself, was *that* all about? Lureen Seldridge enamored with an arrogant chauvinist like Roland Grunnigen when Bryant had said her attitute toward men was based strictly on how much money they had? I didn't believe a word she'd said. Oh, it was easy enough to see why Grunnigen would want to get into bed with her, but I didn't believe for one second he could be in love with her either. Or with anyone else for that matter, except himself. Besides Lureen's beauty, youth, and social position and with what I felt certain was her seductive passion, Grunnigen would hope to eventually snare her into marriage and see himself potentially rich beyond his wildest dreams through her share in the Abbaye.

Outside of a temporary, muscled stallion, however, the pick of which in Lureen's own words she could have at anytime anywhere, what on earth could she possibly see in him?

And why all the anxiety that I shouldn't tell anyone, especially John and Elissa? I thought that was the only part of her performance which was real.

Sitting along in the living room and trying to puzzle it out, I suddenly had a most unpleasant thought, one I didn't care for at all, but I couldn't help it. I was sure Lureen had shown the same come-on sexuality at fifteen that she did now. Behind his aloof haughtiness, John was an emotionally explosive and temperamental man. Had there been anything between them other than his concerned parenthood to cause his angry reaction to her behavior? Lureen had virtually said there was, but if so, it didn't seem possible it could continue with Elissa in the picture. Certainly, I'd had no indication from him of any continuing interest in Alice. Some dangerous liaisons, however, I knew were easily forgotten while others were almost impossible to ever give up completely. And Lureen, beautiful, younger, and with far greater sexuality than poor Alice, was present in John's life every day.

JOHN AND ELISSA were back from San Francisco by the time I went down to breakfast the next morning. They told me that Bryant's financier friend had wanted just about everything they would ever earn for the next twenty years in exchange for getting the banks off their backs.

"It's highway robbery," Elissa said, "but if nothing else comes up, we'll have to do it. It might be our only chance."

Meanwhile, I learned another winery had bought their entire crop of unpicked grapes. "They're coming this afternoon with their own machinery, mechanical picker, trucks and gondolas," Elissa said. "It'll keep the wolf from the door this year, but that's about all."

She and John went off, and I decided to telephone Cloudsmith and report on the meeting with Turbo. I was also eager for any inside police information I might get from him, no matter how meager.

Cloudsmith himself answered and when I related how I'd conquered the Turbo fortress, he fairly cackled with glee. "Bognor probably won't bother you anymore, then," he declared.

"How so?"

"He's had you tailed. Told me yesterday morning you were off someplace."

I thought of how easily I'd driven out the Abbaye's guarded front gates and mentally kicked myself for not realizing that's exactly what Bognor would do.

"By this time," Cloudsmith continued, "he will have added things up and decided you might be more of a problem than you're worth. Turbo swings a lot of weight in this state with people Bognor has to answer to. Both the attorney general and the governor are personal friends. He contributed heavily to their political campaigns."

He wanted to know everything I'd learned. I told him about Alice trying to get Marcel's backing to buy out John but I didn't break Marcel's confidence that he'd had an affair with her. And I told him about old Simon Seldridge changing his will. After that something in me began to balk. Cloudsmith was getting considerable input from me while now I was getting little from him. When I asked about police progress, he told me that the police had nothing new to report. Was the wily old newsman holding out on me for some reason?

Some of my annoyance must have surfaced when I mentioned my idea that Alice might have been killed because she was seen as threatening competition. "Tell that to your friend Bognor," I said.

He reacted quite sharply. "Bognor's no friend of mine," he shot back.

Finishing our conversation on this inconclusive note, I was left to wonder and to try to add up where things stood. I decided once again I could think best if I went for a run, so I geared up for it and left the house. I walked up the drive and the officer at the gates gave me a good looking over, but said nothing as I passed through and onto the silent road ahead.

Usually, running helps me come up with ideas and this time was no exception. I'd hardly gone half a mile when I suddenly realized that there was an aspect to all three murders which I hadn't seriously thought of before, even though now it seemed so obvious I wondered why not. The very savagery of the killings, I felt, indicated something more than just greed as a motive. Someone killing for money poisoned or shot or garroted or sometimes bombed. They didn't do what had been done to Garcia-Sanchez, Hester, and Alice. There was seething rage or hatred there, pent-up fury. Perhaps even a hideously deranged mind.

The day was warm but I felt a cold chill run through me. Bryant had said "be careful" and Marcel had told me he thought I was up against a vicious psychopath. And I was puzzled, too, because if I was right, it seemed to indicate that all three murders had been done by the same person. Yet, I was certain that they had not been.

Almost as I thought this, I was startled by the sudden blaring horn of a pickup truck which pulled alongside. Turning slightly as I ran, I found myself looking into the big red mustachioed moon face of none other than Harry Charwood.

I stopped. He braked.

Although only a few feet from me, he bellowed out from the truck's cab as though I were a mile off. "There she is. Just the lovely little lady I wanted to see."

Without further ado, he climbed down out of the truck's cab. A huge sweating slab of a male, he seemed to take up more of the road than his truck. I fought back an impulse to start running again, if for no other reason than the "lovely little lady." I knew I could easily outdistance him, but I thought better of it. For all I knew he was the murderer, and someone who could easily run me down with his truck. One person had already died that way and there was no one else on the road at that moment but us.

"Look here," he shouted. "Seldridge has a head like a rock. He won't talk to me. He won't come to the phone and the fool police won't let me into the Abbaye. And I can't get through to his brother either. I want you to give them both a message."

"I'll try," I said. "What is it?"

"I've got a perfect solution to his problem," he said. "And mine. Here it is. If they're too thick-headed to sell me the whole Abbaye, I'll settle for renting the hilltop acres. Better a half-loaf than starve to death, right?" A great shout of laughter. "Tell them I'll put it into vines and do a share-cropper deal, give them fifty percent of the profit on every year's harvest. Bryant can keep them afloat until things get going—he's got lots of money—then they'd get to pay off their loans and I'd still get halfway rich selling the grapes to one of the biggies like the Gallo brothers or Turbo."

It was quite a comedown from trying to buy the whole Abbaye. It even sounded like such a fair business deal that it bordered on an offer of help. I could hardly believe my ears.

"Well?" Charwood shouted. "What do you think? Good business for all concerned, no? That's what makes a fair deal, I say. Tell the Seldridges I'll want a six-year lease with an option to renew. That gives me three years to get the vines into grapes, any old varietal will do—I'd be growing it so John needn't get a snobby bad conscience—then three years of getting my money back, and after that six years of laughing all the way to the bank. Will you tell them that?"

I don't know what made me say it, but I did. "What about Jaconello?" I asked.

He stared. "Jaconello? What about him?"

"Where does he come into it? Is this deal with you or with him?"

Obviously he hadn't been expecting that. He chewed it over a moment and said, "So, we're back to me fronting for Jaconello, are we?" All traces of buffoonery had vanished.

"Well, aren't you?"

His eyes narrowed. He flushed angrily, got back into his truck, slamming the cab door behind him. "Why don't you ask Jaconello?" he said.

He let this hang and then before I could come up with an answer, the buffoon reappeared and he shouted, "Or better still, when you get through your silly jogging business, come down to my place, have a glass of champagne or two, and I'll show you some photos I took a couple of years ago in Switzerland. They might answer your question about who's fronting for whom. I'll be there the rest of the day. Just let someone know so you won't have to worry about my possibly doing you in!"

I don't know how long I simply stood in the road looking down its emptiness after he had disappeared around a far bend. My thoughts were finally blasted again, this time by the air horn of a Porsche as it tore past. Coming to my senses, I finished my run and made it back to the house, and after I took a shower, I began to seriously mull over what Charwood had said to me about pictures and Jaconello. I decided to take him up on his invitation. Perhaps nothing would come of it but I was at a complete stalemate and who knew?

I had finished dressing when I happened to glance out my window and saw Lureen, as usual wearing almost nothing, just as she dove into the pool. It didn't occur to me to do what I then did until I came out of my room and walked past her door. It was open. Lureen would be at the pool a while, and on a sudden impulse I went into her room.

I don't know what I expected to find. I had no idea of looking for anything in particular. It was a large and expensively furnished room with a lot of framed photos of herself with various men friends, most considerably older than she, in nightclubs, on yachts, at polo matches, and in exciting places like Monte Carlo, Rome, and Paris.

I glanced into her large walk-in closet filled with very expensive designer clothes. Then, I went through the drawers of her bureau.

I found nothing there. I glanced out the window; she was out of the pool and sunbathing. I turned my attention to her secretary desk. And almost immediately ran into something quite unexpected. In a top drawer were several recent tax returns for the Abbaye. Normal enough, she had a right to them now she was a part-owner, and I almost didn't look at them. But I did and couldn't believe what I saw. Completely different figures than those on the returns I'd copied at the office showed the Abbaye with less loss and far greater earnings.

I put the returns back. Which set gave the Abbaye's true financial picture? And why were they different? Was one set a result of preliminary projections, the other a corrected one? Or, I suddenly thought, had one set been doctored? And if so, why?

Downstairs, I left a message with José to tell Elissa I'd gone to see Harry and went out to my car with the feeling that I'd accidentally stumbled onto something important but without knowing why it was.

19

I HAD NO TROUBLE finding Charwood's vineyard and home. I'd passed the sign for it several times on my way to and from the Abbaye. I drove without hurrying down the winding road descending to the flat floor of the valley, and once there, turned into the narrow dirt lane that was Charwood's front drive. Flanked on both sides by tall, big-trunked eucalyptus trees, it was long and narrow and I wasn't really able to see his house down at the end until I was very nearly on top of it.

It caught me quite by surprise. What appeared was the relic of another era, when wine-making first began in the Napa Valley. It was an old wooden-frame Victorian, a two-story sit-up box complete with gingerbread frieze decorating the eaves, tall ground-floor windows on each side of a center front door, and everything badly in need of paint.

The house was surrounded by fully mature linden and English walnut trees, lending the place a gloomy quality not in keeping with Charwood's character. The few flower beds looked badly neglected and the oval shaped parking area in front of the house needed extensive weeding.

A rutted extension of the front drive led to three shabby

old service buildings. Since I didn't see Charwood's pickup at the house, I figure it had to be over there.

When I got out of my car, there was such a deathly silence surrounding me that I immediately had a vague feeling of foreboding and almost found myself wishing I hadn't come. The feeling got worse when I went to the front door. Although it was slightly ajar, I rang the bell anyway, heard it sound somewhere deep within, and got no answer. I rang again, still no response. I then stepped hesitantly into a front hall which disappeared into darkness beyond a narrow stairway with threadbare carpeting. To my right was a living room; to my left the dining room. Glancing into both, I saw furniture as Victorian and as shabby as the house, and paintings and tapestries one could hardly see for the accumulated dust. It certainly seemed that Marcel Turbo had been right when he said Charwood had no money of his own with which to buy out John. I began to wonder where he'd even get the money to pay rent for the hilltop.

I called out hello. My only answer was the sonorous ticking of the hall's grandfather clock. I called again, then deciding Charwood had to be out at one of the service buildings, walked outside and over to them. There seemed to be nobody around and I didn't see his pickup as I'd expected. He'd told me he'd be there. Had he gone on a quick errand? I stood looking about, called again, and when I still received no answer finally decided that when he did return, it would first be to the house so that the best thing would be to wait by my car. If he didn't show up fairly soon, I told myself, I'd leave and arrange to come another time.

As I was about to leave I heard the muffled sound of a running motor, coming from inside one of the three buildings which seemed to be a small garage. I went over, tried to open the door, and found it locked. I called out; nobody answered. I looked up. There was a window just under the eaves but I had no way of reaching it.

A worn footpath led around the side of the little building

to another window, covered with an iron grill and also out of my reach. But just beyond it, I came to a door that wasn't locked. I pulled on it and it opened, but only about an inch and not enough for me to see inside. I called again. Still nobody answered. But I could smell heavy exhaust fumes. The door was fastened in some way from within. Feeling through the crack I located a heavy hook and tried unsuccessfully to undo it. I then got hold of the doorknob and tugged repeatedly until the hook suddenly gave way and the door, which was quite heavy, flew open. I stepped through it and found myself instantly choking. Charwood's pickup was in there, and the fumes from it were overwhelming. The air was blue with them.

I didn't see Charwood and I don't know what made me look under the truck; maybe it was because its rear end was up on blocks so he could work on it. But I did and then I saw him, his legs first, then his upper body wedged in the narrow space between the truck and the wall immediately beyond it.

I thought he'd had a heart attack. I didn't really stop to think further. I rushed first to the liftup garage door, only just able to squeeze between it and the rear bumper of the truck. But I couldn't make it far enough past a trailer hitch to reach the inside handle. I squeezed back, scrambled to the pickup's cab, turned off the motor and then got down and crawled beneath it to Charwood.

Even with the rear end raised, there wasn't much room. I could barely get halfway up onto my elbows and knees and kept banging my head and scraping my back on the pickup's underside. Finally I was able to see that Charwood had an ugly weal across the side of his head. And I knew he hadn't fallen. Someone had struck him. I felt for his pulse. When I couldn't find any, I was sure he was dead until I saw his chest shudder.

I screamed out at him and tried to rouse him, but couldn't. I had to get him to fresh air, I knew, and do it quickly. I considered putting the pickup in reverse and using it like a battering ram against the door, but there wasn't time to get it down off the blocks.

So I decided that the only thing to do was to try to get Charwood back under the truck and maneuver him to that side door. I tried to pull on his shoulders to turn him around, but I couldn't budge him. I crawled back under the truck and began tugging him by his feet. There was oil on the garage floor, and my hands and clothes were covered with it.

By now I was beginning to think I'd never get him out in time to save him. I'd only moved him about a foot, he was so big and heavy. But then I saw the trolley, one of those low flat things with roller-skate wheels that the auto mechanics sometimes use when working on the undersides of vehicles.

I got it over to him and after two attempts, managed to roll him onto it.

I'd begun to feel deathly ill myself from the fumes. My head pounded and nausea rose and choked me. But I managed to turn the trolley around almost fully so Charwood's head would be near the door—when there was a sudden loud scraping sound and the door slammed shut. Then there was a heavy thudding bang against it and I knew someone had wedged it shut.

For an instant I couldn't move for sheer terror. Whoever was out there had tried to kill Charwood and wanted me dead, too.

I threw my weight against the door as hard as I could. Nothing. I found a heavy hammer and tried to smash it open. That didn't work either. Frantic, I remembered the window. It was quite high and I had to get on top of a cluttered workbench to reach it, only to find that it had been painted shut. I smashed in the glass with the hammer, but I couldn't do anything to loosen the metal grill.

I pushed my face against the grill and breathed in fresh air. It was like a drug. I breathed it and breathed it again and again. But the little air coming in the window was hardly going to clear out the garage. Charwood was going to die on the garage floor right in front of my eyes and there was nothing I could do to save him. It was impossible for me to get him up to the window.

I went back down and thought that maybe if I could get him turned around all the way I could push his face up against a narrow crack between the bottom of the door and the threshold, and he could get air that way.

I pulled on his legs, but this time the trolley didn't budge. Something was blocking one of its wheels. I crawled under the truck and first felt, then saw, a heavy iron ring lying flat in a recess in the floor. One trolley wheel had slipped down in against it. The ring could only mean one thing, a hatch of some sort.

I pulled on the ring as hard as I could, and a heavy slab of cement stirred. I pulled harder. Even before I managed to move the slab away from the dark hole it covered, I could feel the wave of cool air coming up through it.

I got under the truck to look into the hole and saw a ladder to a dirt floor below and then, by the faint glow of an electric light, I saw wine barrels. I was looking into Harry Charwood's cellar.

There was no way I could get Charwood down the ladder, but I turned the trolley back around so that his head hung over the opening. I climbed down the ladder and words can't describe my relief to be out of the garage. I wanted to sit down and just breathe the cellar's cool air, but I had to get help. I made it slowly through the dimly lit aisle between the barrels, holding onto them for support, until I reached a wooden stair. It wasn't far; the cellar was not large. Perhaps there were only fifty barrels down there and not more than a few thousand bottles. I got up the stair, pushed open a door, and found myself in a very big room in another building which, from the cobwebby pipes and unused vats I saw, I knew was once the cuvier.

I looked out a dusty window and through the trees I could

see the house with my car still parked in front of it. It looked a million miles away. Closer by, I saw a door with a sign that said "Office." There would be telephones in both places and I had to phone. I just had to. My life, as well as Charwood's, depended on it.

But I couldn't. Even if I'd somehow found the courage to walk out into the open space where I might well have found myself a helpless target, I simply no longer had the strength to do so. Charwood's weight and his pickup's exhaust fumes had finally taken their toll. My legs suddenly buckled.

I sat down in a heap and stared helplessly, waiting for whoever was out there to come in.

20

BUT NO DANGER came through the door. Unknown to me when I'd gone down into the wine cellar, I'd triggered a security sensor. Charwood's alarm system alerted the sheriff's office in St. Helena, and when the door burst open, minutes later, it was two young sheriff's deputies, their revolvers drawn. I told them that Charwood was in the garage and badly hurt and they went and pulled him out.

He was still alive. An ambulance soon arrived and took him away to a hospital.

I was all right. I only needed a little time to pull myself together and get rid of the poisonous exhaust fumes in my system. But I've never felt such a mess. All I could think of was a hot shower. I didn't get it for a while, though. Instead, I got Bognor who, alerted by the sheriff's deputies, arrived on the scene in record time and immediately began to question me.

I was rescued by Elissa. She'd called the Abbaye to see if there were any messages for her, and José had told her I'd gone to see Charwood. On her way back across the valley, she'd seen a police car turn down Charwood's drive. She drove up to the house, got out of her jeep, took one look at me, heard about three words from Bognor, and simply tore into him. I couldn't believe what she said. Or what she did. I don't think he could either. I've never seen a woman so angry. She screamed at him that he was a first-class son of a bitch and a lot of other things and pushed him violently away from me, and when an officer rather hesitantly tried to interfere, shoved him to one side, too.

White with rage, she told Bognor she was going to make it her personal mission to see he was relieved of his job if it took her the next ten years to do so. And she got away with this. Bognor must have thought it wise to let the whole situation cool. He curtly told me I was free to go.

Elissa drove me home and sent an employee down to collect my rented car. After a wonderful shower, I met her in the living room where she poured me a stiff drink.

"John and I have had it with that bastard," she said. "So has Bryant and he's talked to both the district attorney and the sheriff. Bognor is being pulled out of the Abbaye tomorrow so at least we won't have him or his men camped out in the winery anymore. They'll only come up during the day and just for further forensic examination."

Then she dropped Bognor and focused on me. "Now, tell me. What on earth were you doing down there at Harry's?"

The question seemed guileless enough. But I was chasing down a murderer. Regardless of Elissa coming to my rescue, an inner voice still told me to keep what I was doing and why to myself. "He asked me," I said, "and I decided it was a good chance to see how someone who was just a grower operated."

But Elissa had every right to know about Charwood's offer to lease her unused acreage, and I went on at once to tell her.

Her reaction was first to look thoroughly surprised, then to laugh guardedly and with what I thought was a certain understandable embarrassment. Harry Charwood was, after all, someone she'd always regarded as a clown. "I'll believe it," she said, "if Harry doesn't change his mind and can actually find the rent. Of if somebody doesn't try to kill him again. Who on earth do you suppose it was? And why? It couldn't be Jaconello. Harry's fronting for him. He'd hardly have Harry done in, would he?"

"We don't know Harry's Jaconello's man," I said.

Elissa waved an impatient hand. "Oh, of course he is," she insisted stubbornly. "Unless you think there's somebody else after us we don't know about. Somebody who saw Harry's offer as a threat."

It was exactly what I thought but I didn't want her to know that. I evaded. "What do you think?" I asked.

"That could be it," she said. "Harry's got an awfully big mouth. He probably told a lot of people he was going to bail us out and make our fortune." She smiled wryly and shook her head. "Harry Charwood. I can't believe it."

And then, she abruptly changed her line of thought. She focused on me again. "Margaret, you could have been killed down there along with Harry. Don't you think you ought now to say good-bye to this place? Bryant is certain he can get Bognor to stop holding you here."

I remained cautious and produced an excuse for wanting to stay that I'd had ready for some time. "I need to do a little more research on Napa Valley geology and climate," I said. "Could you possibly bear with me for a few more days?"

If this wasn't what she wanted to hear, I saw no sign of it. She gave me the warmest of smiles. "Margaret, you're welcome to stay, of course, if you really want to. But do you really think you should after everything that's happened here?"

Was she sincere? Her whole manner had surprised me from the moment she appeared to rescue me from Bognor, and I wondered if I was finally seeing the real Elissa that had to lie behind the wine maker and the film star.

She had asked the hospital to call her as soon as Charwood regained consciousness. They did and reported that he had no idea who had struck him down. The nature of the cut on his head indicated the blow had come from behind. I made up my mind then and there to confront the reclusive Jaconello.

Once I did, I wasted no time. I packed an overnight change of clothes along with my flight gear—oxygen mask, helmet, nylon flight suit, gloves, and some maps of California I'd brought along for ballooning—and set out early in the morning. And again, I decided to keep my intentions where murder was concerned to myself. I told Elissa I was going to do some aerial photography of vineyards and that I would be back in two days.

My destination, a long day's drive down half the length of giant California, was the fifty-bedroom imitation Rhineland castle Alfonse Jaconello called home and which he had agressively named Mein Konigreich, My Kingdom. Rumored to have cost as much as a small city to build, it sat in the middle of a ten-thousand acre wilderness at the foot of the San Rafael Mountains, some thirty miles north of Santa Barbara and about fifty miles inland from the coast.

Before leaving I'd checked with a journalist friend in Los Angeles to make certain that the reclusive and aging billionaire was in residence. He was and I arrived just after sundown at a motel by Lake Cachuma near the vineyard country around Los Olivos and Santa Ynez.

In the morning, I drove to a small airfield about ten miles distant. This was not your ordinary airfield, however. Its one runway was grass and the only planes which took off and landed there were, for the most part, open cockpit biplanes whose sole function was to tow gliders airborne. I had taken up gliding after becoming proficient in ballooning. I belong to a club and have built up a respectable number of hours. A call to the field manager and president of the local glider club had reserved me a glider which was waiting for me when I arrived. I geared up, strapped on a backpack parachute, and wedged myself down into the cramped cockpit, closing the bubble canopy over my head. Five minutes later I was airborne.

Like ballooning, gliding is a very special aerial sport. Once you pull the red cable release handle in the cockpit, freeing you from the tow plane at around five hundred feet, you are on your own in an almost silent world. Motorless with only your understanding of weather, especially local conditions, you "feel" your way skyward on thermals, buoyant columns of rising warm air, sometimes to great heights and often for considerable distances. Gliders have reached over thirty thousand feet and have traveled nearly a thousand miles as the crow flies.

With my air speed at about sixty knots, I almost immediately found a thermal off the end of the runway. I spiraled around on it and it carried me slowly up to a thousand feet where I soared for several minutes until I found a second and stronger thermal. Air, moving up the side of the mountains to the east, pulled me across the wide San Joaquin Valley and I climbed continuously. At five thousand feet I picked up the narrow eastward road from Los Olivos that I knew led to Jaconello's Mein Konigreich. Twice I saw other gliders. One came close enough for the pilot to wave and I fervently wished both of them as far from me as possible. I definitely did not want company.

It was now eleven-thirty and for another half an hour, I let myself enjoy the sheer pleasure of flight. Then I finally spotted Jaconello's extraordinary edifice. It looked enormous with its wide cobbled forecourt facing the valley, its many roofs, spires, and turrets, and its acres of outbuildings including the several museums he'd had built for his various collections of art and statuary.

I caught a thermal up to seventy-five hundred feet, but even from there I was able to see the high electric fence barely disguised by hedges of various evergreens which surrounded the entire property. It was like the fence around a prison. Every quarter of a mile, there was a small steel tower topped by closed-circuit security cameras and searchlights. At the main entrance were antlike figures I was certain were uniformed guards.

To my relief, the layout of the castle and its immediate

grounds appeared the same as I'd seen in photographs. The castle stood at the mountainside beginning of a wide flat table, or mesa, of ground. On this there was a great eighteenth-century formal garden, a long center lawn flanked by geometrically shaped flower beds enclosed by low hedges of boxwood, each dominated by large and authentic Greek and Roman statues in heroic postures.

I soared quietly over all of it, lifted up over the hills leading into the mountains behind, then turned and came back and began a slow spiraling descent.

The wind was off the mountains and a few minutes later I came in for my landing over the end of the lawn, winging up its long green length between the statues until I touched down and skidded to a stop with my glider's nose not more than a few yards from the castle's forecourt.

A half-dozen security guards immediately surrounded the cockpit of the little sailplane, and one, looking more ferocious than the rest, tried to pull open the bubble canopy to get at me.

I beat him to it, opened it myself, and got slowly out of the cockpit. Hemmed in at once, I unhooked my parachute, ignoring questions as to what I was doing there, and finally, to their surprise, because I think they apparently just presumed I was a man, took off my helmet and shook out my hair.

There was a moment's dead silence when I did and I was enjoying this little feminine triumph when the guards, who'd been joined by a small crowd of gardeners and groundsmen and even some of the household staff, suddenly parted like the Red Sea before Moses and I found myself confronted by the ugliest octogenarian with the sourest expression on the lumpiest face I'd ever seen. He'd been brought in a wheelchair down a ramp next to the wide marble steps descending from the huge sculpted doors of the castle's main entrance. Now he rose up out of the chair to be assisted the few final steps to me by a covey of male staff. The test of my ruse was about to take place.

21

His first words were simply "And just who do you think you are, please?" The cultured tone was about as imperiously hostile as one could imagine.

Obviously he was a bully, so I decided to give it right back to him. "I might ask you the same," I snapped.

An expression of absolute incredulity came over his face. "You don't know who you're talking to?" he sputtered.

"No, I don't," I said. "But if you're in charge here, which you seem to be, would you mind asking this crowd to move back a little. They could easily damage my glider and I've had rather a bad time of it just now and don't feel like being hemmed in."

He ignored the request. "This is not an airfield," he insisted. "Why are you here and who are you?"

"I'm Margaret Barlow," I answered crisply, "and I'm here because I had to make a forced landing. Something seemed to be blocking my controls."

I held my breath a little at that one. If anyone had decided to test me, he had only to seize an aileron or the glider's rudder and, moving it about, quickly discover that there was nothing wrong at all. "If I may use your telephone," I went on, "I'd like to call the airfield so they can send a truck up to bring the glider back. There's no way I can take off in it again. Then, if it doesn't inconvenience you, I'll just sit by and wait." I glanced pointedly at my watch. "I'm sure I must have interrupted your lunch."

His reply was to continue to stare at me, incredulous. Then, to my astonishment, his lumpy features broke into what I can only describe as a secretively sly smile. "I am not lunching for another few minutes and I will expect you to join me. I'm Jaconello, Mrs. Barlow. Alfonse Jaconello."

It was not an invitation. It was an order and without further word, he turned for his wheelchair, staff scrambling to assist him into it and then wheel him in silence back up the ramp and into the castle.

I heaved a silent sigh of relief and, savoring my triumph, put my parachute in the cockpit of the sailplane and closed down the canopy. "Now," I said, "if someone would kindly show me to the telephone."

An elderly man who I presumed from his dress and slightly superior air was some sort of major domo or a private secretary stepped forward and said, "This way, madam, please."

I followed him across the cobbled forecourt and up the marble steps into a huge hall. A copy of a Roman atrium, it was as big as a good-sized church and several stories high. Its walls were Italian marble, its flooring worn Roman mosaics. High above, the frescoed ceiling was clearly the work of some Renaissance master. Off it, I was shown to a mirrored and marble powder room which would have done justice to the most expensive hotel. It had a telephone without a dial, a precautionary measure, I guessed, against employees calling friends around the world. A most courteous operator somewhere in the bowels of the castle answered and placed my call for me, and, after making arrangements with the airfield, I rejoined the elderly secretary who had been awaiting my return. He led me through several large reception rooms where there were crystal chandeliers and mirrored walls, then down a long wide gallery hung with a collection of important French impressionists, and finally into a perfectly immense dining room where the dark paneling was festooned with magnificent antlered hunting trophies.

The long mahogany table which easily would have sat thirty-six persons was set only for two. Jaconello's place was at the head and he was already there occupying a massive armchair. A second place had been set for me at reasonable conversational distance. A liveried footman in white breeches and blue swallowtail jacket with gold trim and gold tassled epaulettes stood behind each chair. As I went to mine, I quickly took in the extraordinarily beautiful luncheon service, each plate with a different hand-painted medieval hunting scene, and the crystal wine goblets with their heavy gold bases.

Seated, I made the necessary appropriate noises of appreciation for the hospitality. Jaconello accepted this in dead silence, staring at me with watery eyes and no expression.

We were served immediately. I began to compliment him on the appearance of the food and then he came to life. With a vengeance. "Skip all that," he suddenly barked. "And no more nonsense about a forced landing. I used to fly myself and there's nothing at all wrong with your controls. I watched you land. Why are you really here?"

I was caught flat-footed. I remembered the secretively sly smile on his face when he'd asked me to join him for lunch and realized now that I'd been outsmarted. I had, I knew, but seconds to come up with something and beating about the bush wasn't going to work. The man was a pirate who hadn't amassed a fortune manipulating financial markets by being stupid. Having caught me out once, he would see through any lie. The one thing I had to hide was my connection with the Seldridges. If he was indeed after the Abbaye, revealing that would have to make him hopelessly distrustful of me.

"Well?" he demanded.

"You're right, of course," I admitted. "A fake landing was the only way I could think of to get through your security. I wanted to see you."

"What about?"

"I'm a photo-journalist, Mr. Jaconello, and no, I don't want your picture or pictures of your castle. As you can see I am without a camera. I came to California from the East to do a story about wine in general but soon decided a more interesting story would be one about a particular winery producing an estate vintage to compete with the best French château *premier cru*."

"Well, you don't need me for that," he said. "There are already several vineyards out here producing great wines."

"Exactly," I agreed. "Enough of them, I've discovered, to lessen the story's impact. Unless, however, it has a special angle. You, for example. The rumor is that you are trying to buy yourself a vineyard in order to produce just such a wine."

"Nonsense."

"It isn't nonsense," I retorted. "And you know it. You're Swiss, your family made wine from a small vineyard in the Lake Geneva region. French winemakers disdain the Swiss and their wine. It would be the most natural thing in the world for a man of your wealth and pride to enjoy a little revenge by producing a better product. And if that's the case, I, for one, hope you succeed."

Then I thought, it's now or never, and plunged into deep water. "Rumor also has it that a certain Harry Charwood is fronting for you in your search for the right vineyard."

He stared at me, instantly hostile. "Nobody fronts for Jaconello! Harry who?"

"Charwood," I repeated.

I waited while he made a pretense of remembering Charwood. Or was it a pretense? I suddenly wasn't sure. His hesitation seemed real.

"Charwood . . . Charwood . . ." he mused. "Never heard of him."

"He's a big man. With red hair and a very loud voice."
He shook his head. "No."

I persisted. "So he's definitely not working for you."

It was as far as I had to go. Unexpectedly, and for just an instant, he let his guard down.

"Work for me? What are you after, young lady? I know every one who ever worked for me. He doesn't and never has."

The unexplained venom both in his eyes and his tone told me at once, however, that there was surely something between them.

I didn't get a chance to think much further. Jaconello simmered a moment, then, and with naked suspicion, demanded "When does this story appear? What magazine?"

"I don't know," I replied. "I'm freelance and the story is my idea."

He was silent again, brooding over the nearly untouched food on his plate. "Take this away," he said suddenly and very unpleasantly to a butler who was standing by at silent attention. "I'll have an omelette. And don't be all day. I haven't forever."

When his plate was hurriedly removed, he turned to me again and said, "If ever I should decide to establish a vineyard, your best source of information would be my public relations firm." He mentioned a well-known organization in New York. And then with yet another sly smile, he asked, "How long have you been gliding?"

And that was that. There was nothing to do but retreat gracefully. During the rest of lunch, and I'm sure just to put me in my place, he made certain I knew of his most important financial successes. Then afterward, he insisted on taking me on a tour of the castle to make certain I fully appreciated what those successes had provided. Eventually, the chief security guard came to say that the truck had arrived from the airfield and was loading my glider aboard. The truck was also my ride back and I had to go.

In his wheelchair, Jaconello escorted me through the great

center hall to the huge doors leading out to the forecourt, I think only to ensure himself that I really did leave. It was because he did that that my whole adventure suddenly took a completely different turn and became worthwhile.

Almost at the end of the hall we passed an open door to a room which I took to be Jaconello's private study. Glancing in I saw something which suddenly provoked in me a wild hunch about something.

I stopped and said, "Oh, Mr. Jaconello, your study. How very impressive!"

I had nothing to lose and went right in. He at once followed. At first I purposefully ignored what I'd seen and just looked around. The room had a beautiful view out over the formal front lawn with its statuary and gardens, but otherwise was oppressively somber with a vast Victorian desk, heavy ornate furniture, and dark drapes. It was also filled with a lifetime of mementos. And reflecting the power and wealth Jaconello had accumulated by manipulating the world's financial markets, there were dozens of photos of Jaconello with royalty and presidents at one point or another in his life. I made appropriate comments and he boasted about the prime ministers of Europe who he said were indebted to him.

Then I turned to what I'd seen from the door and the reason for my hunch. Hanging on a wall was a large group photo taken in a vineyard with a background of snowcapped mountains above what I recognized as Lake Geneva. I knew now from Jaconello's reaction at lunch that there definitely was something between him and Harry Charwood, and Harry had said he took pictures in Switzerland, insinuating they would show me who was really fronting for Jaconello. Could this be one of them?

I looked at the photograph closely. There were a dozen people of various ages in the posed group, most of them clearly Swiss peasants. Two who were not immediately caught my eye. One was Jaconello and from the way he looked the photo was a fairly recent one.

The other person proved my hunch right beyond my wildest hopes. My heart suddenly pounded with an excitement I was hard put not to show.

"These must be your Swiss vineyards and your family there," I said as casually as I would. "What nice-looking people and what a lovely place to grow up."

Jaconello grunted noncommittally and I pointed to the person next to him. "And what a handsome young man. Is he a relative, too?"

He fell for it. "My nephew," he said. "But if he expects to get any of this," he waved vaguely at the vast castle, "he's going to have to prove to me he's worth it."

The young man in the photo was Roland Grunnigen.

Back in the hall, I again thanked Jaconello for his hospitality and said I'd be in touch with his PR people. He simply nodded dismissively and was wheeled away.

I went down to the waiting truck, on which my glider, wings removed and neatly stowed, had been loaded, and was greeted by the airfield manager who had come out himself with a driver. He wasn't very happy about my "forced landing." I told him the truth which went over far better. We had chili and cold beer for dinner with some other pilots at a local roadside restaurant outside Los Olivos, and in the morning, I headed back for the Napa Valley.

22

ON THE WAY BACK up the long Cental Valley with its mile after mile of vegetable and fruit farms and vineyards, a number of things were suddenly clear to me. Jaconello, by refusing to discuss it, had virtually admitted he wanted a superior estate winery and unquestionably the Abbaye, a strangely vindictive personal ambition, I thought, for a man who could buy half the Napa Valley if he wished.

People's lives meant nothing to the old man. I was certain he had ordered his nephew to sabotage the Abbaye and knew, equally, that Grunnigen was then almost assuredly guilty of murdering Garcia-Sanchez. I mentally kicked myself for not having seen the connection between him and Jaconello long before this. Grunnigen's odd way of speaking French was the very distinctive manner the Swiss spoke the language in the French part of their country.

If Lureen knew Grunnigen was Jaconello's nephew, that surely would explain her involvement with him. He stood to inherit a vast fortune if he proved his merit to his uncle by delivering the Abbaye. I remembered the faintly amused smile Lureen wore when Elissa and Hester sparred before dinner the fateful night of Hester's murder. If she already knew of the offer Hester's brewer was making, she also knew that Jaconello, once appraised of it, would top it at once.

Her knowledge might also explain the inflated tax returns I'd found in her desk. By making the Abbaye seem to be worth much more than it was, Jaconello could be persuaded to increase his purchase offer so substantially that the Seldridges might simply no longer be able to say no. Grunnigen would then be assured of his uncle's approval and thus his inheritance.

Could Lureen also know Grunnigen had killed Garcia-Sanchez? Possibly, I thought, if Grunnigen had been foolish enough to tell her. The life of a poor migrant Mexican worker could hardly have meant any more to her than it would have to Jaconello.

But where did Harry Charwood fit in? Remembering the venom in Jaconello's eyes when I'd introduced Harry's name, I was certain the Swiss hated him far more than was warranted by any ordinary threat to his ambitions.

Suddenly, I realized what it must be. Blackmail! What a perfect set up for it! Obviously Charwood knew that Grunnigen was Jaconello's nephew and that Grunnigen was a safe bet to be both the saboteur and a murderer. And blackmail fitted Harry's character. Where I hadn't been able to see him as a murderer, I had no problem picturing him holding a pistol to someone's head and bellowing with laughter as he did. By threatening to expose Grunnigen and thus implicate Jaconello himself, he could have demanded an extortionist's commission from the reclusive billionaire for persuading the Seldridges to sell. And if the Seldridges now accepted his current offer not to buy but to rent, this money would also come from Jaconello. Small wonder the Swiss hated him so. Harry would have trapped him into rescuing for the Seldridges the very property Jaconello so compulsively coveted.

Turning off onto the narrow road which led across the Napa Valley and then wound up the hill to the Abbaye, I slowed as I approached Charwood's vineyards. And when

I got to his entrance, I stopped. Looking up the long dirt drive that led to his old Victorian house, I wondered if I shouldn't try to get into it and find the photographs and possibly even some of Charwood's bank statements which might show unexplained deposits and help prove he was a blackmailer. I knew I should go to the police but I didn't relish the idea of facing Bognor without hard evidence to back me up.

My courage failed me, however. It was getting close to sundown, shadows were long across Charwood's vineyards, and the thought of entering his gloomy house after what had happened to me there proved too much. I drove on and almost reached the Abbaye when a familiar station wagon bore down on me. Getting close, it flashed its lights for me to stop. I did and John and Elissa pulled alongside.

"Bryant's gone and smashed himself up in that damned car of his," John said. "A hospital in San Francisco just called."

Elissa spoke across him from the passenger seat. "Margaret, we'll call and let you know how he is."

I continued on to the house, acutely anxious about Bryant. But then, as I drove through the now unguarded front gates, that anxiety gave way to another and quite different one. It suddenly occurred to me that Jaconello might have checked up on me after I left, perhaps discovered I was staying at the Abbaye, and then contacted his nephew. Bognor had removed his investigative headquarters elsewhere and I was very alone at the Abbaye. To have any peace of mind, I needed to know where Grunnigen was.

I was met in the front hall by José, who told me dinner would be in twenty minutes. "There'll be just you and Miss Lureen," he said.

We chatted somberly a moment about Bryant's accident, then I said, "Where is Mr. Grunnigen, José?"

Lureen answered that herself. Neither José nor I had heard her come silently down the stairs while we talked. "He's gone to Napa for the evening," she said. "Why?"

I covered as quickly as I could. "Elissa asked me, if I saw

him, to tell him about Bryant," I said and added, "if he hadn't already heard. I met her and John coming up the hill."

"I told him," she said, going on into the living room without another word.

The thought of eating alone with Lureen was not inspiring. I hardly had enough confidence in her to reveal what I'd learned about Grunnigen. Whether she already knew or not how criminal he was, she might well decide Jaconello's money was worth more than my life, somehow contact him, and bring him back to the Abbaye.

When I went to the dining room, she was already seated at the table and reading a celebrity gossip magazine. "I hope your uncle isn't badly hurt," I said, taking my chair.

She didn't look up. "He's not my uncle," she said. Her tone was a blend of hostility, resentment, and boredom.

My sense of danger abruptly heightened. This wasn't the same Lureen who had tearfully pleaded with me not to reveal her affair with Grunnigen. Did Grunnigen and she indeed know I'd seen Jaconello? Common sense told me to get in my car and leave, right then. I didn't. Instead I decided my only course was to play innocent. "Bryant, then," I said.

She didn't reply. José appeared with a delicious gazpacho soup and asked me if I would like wine. I said yes and he brought in some cold Chardonnay. The soup was followed by a Mexican meal of burritos and tamales which under the circumstances I was hard put to enjoy. I made a few abortive attempts to converse which elicited no response other than the odd muttered sound, so I gave up and we ate in silence.

When dessert came, José asked us if we'd like coffee on the terrace. "It's quite warm tonight," he said.

I said yes, but Lureen had her head buried in the magazine so I went out by myself.

The sun had long set and night was rushing in with the first stars appearing in the west. The air was perfumed with the scent of pine, eucalyptus, and night-blooming jasmine. I thought of the almost perfect beauty of the Abbaye setting, the refuge it should be from the tensions of the world outside. Instead, it had become a place of horror, permeated by fear, and I wondered if it would be forever tainted by everything that had happened.

To my surprise, I'd hardly seated myself when Lureen came out with her magazine, and, with a continued air of acute boredom, sat down, lit a cigarette, and stared off into space. Then, just to double my anxiety, José brought out the coffee, said good night, and told us he was off to a movie in St. Helena.

I was just listening to the now familiar putt-putt-putt of his little moped going up to the front gate when Lureen rose and said, "The pool has to be covered, otherwise it collects bugs and gets cold from the night fog."

She headed for one end of it and for a large nylon tarpaulin rolled up around a brass axle extending about foor feet past each of the pool's sides. When she reached it, she turned and said, "It takes two."

"Oh, of course," I said and went to join her. By the time I got there she had grasped a corner of the tarpaulin and was waiting for me to do the same. Her expression was petulant. It was clearly a job she hated and I asked if it was always her responsibility.

"No," she said. "Not if John or Elissa are here and if they aren't, I only do it if I can get José or somebody to help."

I went around to the other side of the pool and got hold of the opposite corner and we began to walk along the pool's edge, pulling the tarpaulin with us so that as it slowly unrolled from the axle it covered the water.

The tarpaulin made a heavy scraping sound as it dragged over the cement surface, but I think it wasn't until we were halfway down the pool's length that my memory registered and I identified it. It was exactly the sound I had heard the night Hester was murdered.

I must have stopped dead with the recognition because I heard Lureen say, "What's wrong?"

I came to my senses. "Nothing," I replied. And hauled at

the tarpaulin again. But there was a great deal wrong. Grunnigen had not been at the house that fatal evening, and José had long since gone to bed in his utility building apartment. There'd been only four of us there: myself and Lureen, John and Elissa. It took two people to cover the pool, I'd just learned that, and now I knew almost certainly that John and Elissa had done it and that neither had been in the shower as I'd supposed when I'd gone to fuss with my door lock and had seen Lureen head for the back stairs to the kitchen.

For Lureen had just told me she never covered the pool if John and Elissa were there to do it. Besides that, I'd heard the strange scraping sound almost as soon as I'd returned to bed and, with the kitchen some distance away, it would have been next to impossible for her to get out to the pool so quickly.

So why had the shower been running? I could think of only one explanation: Lureen had left it on all along to make it look as though she was there when she wasn't. She'd been on her way back from somewhere, planning to turn it off, and when I appeared, had thought quickly and gone down the stairs to hide that she'd just come up them.

Where had she been, then? And why the deceit?

I felt my blood run cold. I couldn't be right. Hester was her mother.

But then something unexpected happened and almost immediately told me that yes, I could be. I heard the distant but heavy rattle of the utility building's big garage door opening. Looking over, I saw a man standing in the garage's bright light.

Roland Grunnigen closed the door behind him, and was hidden from me by the night.

I could hardly breathe. I could hear my own heart beating as I said to Lureen, "You told me Roland was in Napa."

She smiled. It was a horrible, spiteful smile. "I guess I told you wrong."

23

SOME THINGS REMAIN fixed forever as indelible photographs in the album of one's memory. One I will always preserve is Lureen, in the gathering California twilight, staring back at me from the other side of the swimming pool at the Abbaye. To my keyed-up imagination I felt she could read my every thought about her.

The pool covered, she turned without a word and went back to her chair, holding her magazine up to the light from the living room and sipping the last of her coffee. I muttered some excuse and left the terrace, trying to appear as casual as I could. There wasn't time any longer to try to think things out and to understand motives. I'd come as far as I could on my own. Now I needed help.

I decided at once against the telephone in the alcove between the living room and the front hall and went quickly to Elissa and John's room where there was another. I reached it, dialed the operator and told her I had an emergency and needed the police. It seemed forever before a crisply authoritative female voice answered and even longer when she insisted I give my name and where I was calling from before I was allowed to say anything else. In a half-whisper, I finally told her please to notify Captain Bognor that there was serious trouble at the Abbaye de Ste. Denise and to come at once. Infuriatingly, this faceless person wanted to know what sort of trouble.

Somewhere in the middle of my frantically telling her Bognor already knew what kind of trouble, I heard the click of a telephone receiver. Someone was listening in on my end, I was sure. Grunnigen? Or Lureen?

Whichever, they knew now that I was someone who'd have to be silenced and the only intelligent thing for me to do was leave quickly while I still could. My car keys were in my room. I went up, collected them and my handbag, and headed back for the stairs. The front hall below was empty. I started down cautiously, made it to the front door, then out to my car. I started up the motor, sure its noise would bring Grunnigen on the run, and headed up the driveway for the front gates. I reached into the glove compartment for the little transmitter which would open them.

It wasn't there.

But I'd put it there, I knew I had. I stopped the car, looked in my handbag, then the glove compartment again. It was in neither. I turned on the interior light and searched the car's floor.

Nothing.

I felt under both seats, on the floor in the back. Still nothing.

I turned off the lights. Obviously someone had deliberately taken the transmitter so I couldn't leave the premises. I sat there and desperately tried to think what to do. I couldn't stay in the car, trapped in it. I'd made enough noise to be heard everywhere. They were bound to come. Get out and think afterward, I decided. I opened my door, stepped into what seemed a betraying glare from the car's interior light, and quickly moved into the dark shadow of a big oleander bush. Nothing. Only a terrible silence.

Then I remembered the way into the Abbaye by the chapel, the side door opposite the vestry that Cloudsmith had taken and which Alice had said she and others often used. I didn't need a key, I was going out, not coming in. All I needed was to keep my nerve long enough to get there.

The moon was behind the chapel, its pale light slanting down into the cloister itself and turning the archway entrance into a vague and ghostly shape. The loggia would be dark, pitch-dark. I'd used that darkness once, I could use it again.

The crunch of gravel when I crossed the driveway sounded like thunder and it seemed an eternity until I reached the archway. There were protective shadows along one side. I slipped into them and stood there. So far so good. But where were Grunnigen and Lureen? They had to be someplace. I stood and listened. The darkness could hide them from me as well as me from them. I forced myself to move.

I stole into the inky darkness of the columned loggia and slowly made my way to the chapel, my back to the wall, my right arm extended outward, feeling blindly. I got to the door of the bottling plant but without my little pencil flashlight, the conveyor belt loaded with bottles and the stacks of bottles in crates and boxes would be impossible to avoid. I had no doubt I would crash into them.

I groped on to the door to the office and again hestitated. I could use the phone there, but I couldn't get in without a key and the key was in the telephone alcove.

An eternity passed before I reached the door to the vestry. I felt for the latch and it lifted with the faintest click and the door pushed open easily. The mustiness of the little room, the heavy smell of old adobe and dust, assailed me. It was like a cloth held tight over my nose and mouth.

For what seemed forever, I didn't move. I stood in the darkness and tried to remember the exact layout of the room so I wouldn't bump into furniture. Presently, the room began to take vague form. There was faint light coming through its one small dusty window from the moonlit cloister.

I moved finally, very cautiously, gliding one foot out before the other so as not to trip over anything. I got into the chapel and was immediately aware of another, very faint light, which came from the narrow stairs down to the crypt. It had to be the low-watt bulb at the entrance to the labyrinth of wine cellars. Was there someone there, waiting?

I might have made it if I'd avoided crossing in front of those stairs to get to the door to the outside and instead had gone down the dark center aisle between the pews. But I didn't. I was so close to getting away that I chanced the light and cut in front of it. Then I skirted the dark mass of a confessional box and moved to a window, glancing out at the small parking area and where, in moments, I'd be safe.

And what I saw stopped me cold. With surprise, with astonished disbelief, then with acceptance and overwhelming relief. All of that almost simultaneously. I stook stock-still, a perfect silhouette in front of the window. And stared.

At a car parked not twenty feet away. Outside, there was enough moonlight to see clearly the car's low distinctive lines. Enough to distinguish its silvery gray sleekness.

It was Bryant's Ferrari. I wasn't alone anymore. Bryant was there and he was safety.

But that was impossible. He was in the hospital. He had been in a car accident.

From relief to terror again. Then, shockingly, Lureen's voice, sudden and urgent: "Bryant, quick." And I knew the truth, that Bryant was not safety, that Elissa and John had been enticed away and I'd been set up.

All that went through my mind, again in a second. And my heart turned into a great leadened weight because I knew it was too late.

He stepped from the confessional box right next to me where he'd been hiding, a dark, fast-moving presence. I didn't have the chance to run. Or scream. He was very quick and sure.

His arms wrapped around me in an instant, pinning mine to the sides of my body and one of his hands clamped something over my mouth. It was a cloth of some kind. It was wet and had a burning sickly smell, and I knew at once it was chloroform.

FOR A SECOND I was helpless. Just a second. Every muscle and nerve was water. I couldn't react. And Bryant's hand was so tight over my mouth and nose I couldn't breathe. It was what saved me, his hand, that awful choking smell of chloroform. I could only think: air. I had to have air. Then not thinking at all. My body acting alone, helpless one second, the next, violent. I hunched forward, kicking back with strength. And I bit into his hand. Deep. He cursed, let go, tried to pin me again, unsuccessfully. I had one arm free and I twisted half around and struck backward as hard as I could. The outer edge of my palm caught him across the bridge of his nose. I could feel the crack of it right up to my shoulder. He shouted and let go again and I fled for Cloudsmith's little door, falling, rising, stumbling on.

I didn't make it. He was right behind me, shouting "Quick! Grab her!"

There was a sudden flare of light right in my eyes. A blinding flashlight. Lureen's. It stopped me short. Bryant's forearm locked across my face, but I dropped free before he could pull me into him. I scrambled between two pews for the center aisle and past the light. Lureen's voice:

"I'll get her." She ran between the next pews, alongside of me.

Bryant reached for me once more and what saved me was her blinding him with the light, too. He tripped over something and I made it to the center aisle before either of them.

It all happened quickly. I headed for the vestry, then realized they could easily get me in the cloister. Or Grunnigen might be there. I reached the end of the aisle in front of the altar and didn't know where to turn. Without thinking, I bolted down the steep narrow stairs into the crypt leading into the wine cellars.

It was a crazy thing to do. My idea was that I could get out by the door up to the cuvier; after that, the vineyards. I didn't stop to think that all the exits might be locked. Again, I didn't really think at all. I was trapped and ran for my life straight into another trap.

It was cool down there and smelled of wine and old oak. Cool and dead silent. There was a dim light bulb every once in a while, just enough so I could see my way down a long center cellar. It was traversed twice by two smaller cellars leading to two long side ones which ran beneath opposite sides of the cloister.

I got to one of those traverses before Bryant and Lureen reached the center cellar. They didn't see me turn into it, I was sure of that, but I knew they'd figure it out quickly enough.

Maybe it was fifty feet to where the traverse joined the side celler running under the cuvier. When I reached it, I stopped. The blood pounding in my head was all I could hear. Nothing else. Just that terrible pounding. It was dark; the light bulb had burned out. I had to see which way they'd go and got behind a pyramid of three barrels enabling me to look between them without being seen.

There was the flickering light of a flashlight in the center cellar, finally. First Bryant, then Lureen, came into view. They stopped, trying to guess which way I'd gone, and I saw his vintner's knife The blade was open.

Bryant. Someone I'd trusted and never suspected. Of course, Bryant. The rebellious brother condemned by the unforgiving patriarch. Bryant, murderously jealous of favored John, hiding his hate and seeing justice one day in John's dreams destroyed and himself wealthy beyond most men's powers.

He was a killer and he was going to kill me, had to. I didn't think further. I didn't bother with why. Why he'd murdered Hester and Alice. Or why he wanted me dead. Or where Lureen fitted in, except the way they stood together; the way their bodies communicated told me they'd been together a long time. Grunnigen didn't count or was just being used. They separated, Bryant coming my way.

Where was the door to the cuvier? I couldn't remember. But it couldn't be far and the darkness would help me. The darkness and the scores and scores of barrels I could hide behind.

I groped along and felt the door at last. It was so close I'd almost slipped by.

It was firmly locked.

Time stopped. I went numb. I tried to think, to remember. There were other doors. Had to be. There would be one to the bottling plant. But where? All the way across the cellars, and it might be locked, too. I was standing in the near dark, trying to think, when I saw a shadow on the wall of the cellar where there was more light. It moved. He was coming cautiously my way. I had to run again, take a chance on Lureen.

I ducked into the next traverse, headed back under the cloister for the bottling plant on the other side, made it across the center cellar, and kept going toward the one that ran under the loggia.

Lureen appeared at the junction. She stopped, shone her light about, and I saw just beyond her the rusty iron gate of the Jesuit ossuary. She pointed the light through the bars, then opened the gate to see better, stepping into the ossuary entrance. Her light splashed over the piles of bones and skulls, heaped up almost to the vaulted ceiling.

I glanced back. Bryant was at the far end of the traverse. He spotted me and shouted.

Lureen spun around. I threw myself forward, slamming the gate into her, and she went down backward into the pile of bones, her flashlight flying away.

I ran blindly down the cellar back toward the chapel. But I knew I couldn't outrun them. I stopped by a rack of wine bottles, one reaching up to the ceiling. I squeezed between it and the cellar wall and got my feet up against it and as Bryant caught up, pushed with everything I had.

The rack tottered. Bottles fell. Two, three, a dozen, more. And then it came crashing down, bottles cascading, breaking, splintering, rolling everywhere. Hundreds of them and they half-buried him. But as I clambered away he seized one of my legs. I pulled free, but he caught the other one and I fell. Struggling, he heaved up through the bottles and the only thing that stopped him was the broken bottle with which I wildly struck out.

It caught him across the face.

When a man screams, it's not like a woman. It's something to freeze one's blood. Bryant Seldridge screamed and covered his face with both hands and I got up and saw Lureen almost on me. I stumbled away over loose rolling bottles and broken glass, and ran on toward the crypt.

They came after me, both of them, but I made it up into the darkness of the chapel. All I could think of was the little side door. If I could only just get to it and outside, I'd be able to go into the woods across the road and maybe I'd have a chance there.

But I forgot the pews and rushed headlong into one.

Then they ran into me. And all three of us went down in a heap, Bryant cursing and blinded. All of us in a tangle in the dark. Lureen's flashlight rolled under the pew and light from it glinted on Bryant's knife as he wildly tried to slash me. Then Lureen suddenly shouted "No! Bryant!" and screamed, with her scream beginning to bubble like someone half under water. And Bryant, crazed with pain, slashing and slashing blindly and shouting obscenities at her.

I stumbled to the door and outside into the coolness of the night. But I couldn't run anywhere. Not anymore. I could barely walk. I remembered Bryant's Ferrari and I prayed he'd left the keys in it.

They weren't in the ignition but I found them up behind the sun visor, the same place he'd kept them during Hester's funeral before he'd driven me back to the Abbaye. I had trouble trying to start the motor. Nothing was familiar. It took me forever to find the hand brake and release it. I'd just got the lights on when Bryant came out of the chapel. He was covered with blood now, his face and hands, the whole front of him, Lureen's and his.

I couldn't find the door lock and when he reached the door as I was trying to get the car in gear, he yanked it open and tried to pull me out. I hung on to the wheel, got into a gear and let out the clutch, and we lurched forward, Bryant hanging onto me, his dead weight nearly pulling me out. We rocketed onto the road and I was hitting him to make him let go, desperate, when there was a great flare of light directly in front of me.

It was another car and I ran head-on into it.

An awful crash. Then darkness, the smell of oil. I sat behind the Ferrari wheel, the wheel pushing me back into the seat and the floorboards pushing my legs up against the wheel. I couldn't move. And Bryant wasn't there anymore.

Epilogue

PEOPLE. Lights. A voice asking: "Are you hurt?"

It was Bognor. Cloudsmith was with him and got the scoop of his lifetime. It was the odious chief detective's car that I had smashed into.

Although I looked the worst kind of mess, I suffered nothing more serious than a slightly sprained ankle, exhaustion, and a residue of sheer unrelenting terror. As I was being helped from the Ferrari, Elissa and John arrived, frantic with anxiety after they'd discovered Bryant's "accident" was a hoax.

Cloudsmith busily took photos of everything: of the two totally wrecked cars; of Bryant, lying injured on the road behind them; of Lureen, huddled lifeless in a lake of blood between two pews in the chapel.

He got pictures, too, of Bognor lording it over the whole scene. To my everlasting annoyance, it was the horrid little homicide officer, not I, who first became suspicious of Bryant, although Bognor missed out on Lureen, just as he missed out on Roland Grunnigen. Hearing from Cloudsmith that old Seldridge had changed his will, the chief detective had an analysis done of Simon's signature. Handwriting experts not only revealed it to be a forgery but, checking on John's and Bryant's handwriting, found it was one skillfully done by Bryant himself. The injustice of his brother's being the sole inheritor of the Abbaye and the fortune it represented had proved too much for him. Later, when a series of bad business deals cost him most of his own self-made fortune and threatened him with ruin, he saw selling the Abbaye as a way out.

The unexpected sabotage of two years' wine crops was a gift from Heaven in putting pressure on John to do so. Early on, he became certain Grunnigen was responsible when he recognized, as I finally did, that the viticulturist's odd French accent was Swiss. And then, when checking his alien registration, found that he was Jaconello's nephew. It was to his advantage, however, to keep quiet.

I had little sympathy for Bryant. Out of envy and greed, he'd murdered two women and had tried to kill Harry Charwood. He had twice tried to kill me.

I remained at the Abbaye for another ten days, eating far too much of José's wonderful cooking and slowly putting my nerves back together again. I was deeply touched when I learned the power of Cloudsmith's editorial pen almost overnight raised a substantial sum for the family of Julio Garcia-Sanchez. I spent one lovely sunny afternoon in his company walking around the vineyards and, with the help of Bryant's rambling confession, finally put together for him the facts of the three sordid, coldly premeditated murders.

"Grunnigen killed the poor Mexican," I told him. "Bryant learned that from Lureen. And the forensic lab has now identified, as his, some hair found on the butt of Grunnigen's shotgun."

"But Bryant killed Hester," Cloudsmith said. "Why?"

"She'd discovered his business failures and teamed up with him to force John to agree to sell. But she leaned too hard on him. A suit to break Simon's will would have exposed his forgery."

"Poor John," Cloudsmith said. "His own brother."

"John suspected Bryant, you know," I said. "Right from the beginning. The night of Hester's death, he heard Bryant's Ferrari going down the hill to the valley. It was long after Bryant had left the house. And, as he learned later, well after the time the police said Hester was murdered. When Alice died, he believed Bryant also killed her and he was terrified Bryant would sense that he did and come after him next. I saw real fear on his face when they took Alice away."

We'd reached the top of one of the two hills looking down over the Abbaye, nestled amid its vineyards. Enjoying a moment's rest, I told the old editor about Lureen. As much as I'd been able to piece together, anyway.

"Her liaison with Bryant began when she was barely out of high school," I said. "And at first it was a way of making a slave of someone, a source of power. Then later, she saw that if she married him she'd share his half of the Abbaye along with what she'd get from Hester."

"Until she got involved with Roland Grunnigen."

"Exactly. When Grunnigen foolishly revealed who he was, she saw far bigger money through him from Jaconello."

I told Cloudsmith, also, how Bryant had early on become so obsessed with Lureen that he put up with her many infidelities. "He even found her affair with Grunnigen useful," I explained. "It gave him the opportunity to plant the inflated tax returns I saw in Lureen's bedroom. He knew they'd be passed on to Jaconello and hoped they would entice him into increasing his offer."

"But didn't Bryant realize he might lose her to Grunnigen?"

"Oh, yes. And that was a nightmare he couldn't shake. The lure of a fortune for himself through a sale of the Abbaye was as strong as his obession for her."

Cloudsmith shook his head. "I've known Bryant Seldridge for a long time," he said. "It's hard to imagine him a murderer, let alone murdering so savagely."

"The savagery wasn't so much his," I said. "Or even Grunnigen's. It was Lureen's. She joined in all three murders.

And helped plan them. Catching Garcia-Sanchez on a lonely road was her idea. And so was luring Hester and Alice to the winery at night. You have to go back a long way to understand her," I went on. "She developed a psychotic hostility toward the whole world beginning right from childhood when she was abandoned by Hester and all the time she was growing up, and finally when John married Elissa, which she saw as the ultimate rejection. It eventually all burst out when Garcia-Sanchez threatened what she hoped to get from Jaconello, then when Hester's possible purchase of the Abbaye appeared an equal threat. And again when she saw a new danger in Marcel Turbo."

"How did she find out about him?"

I smiled, remembering the faint click I'd heard on the telephone when calling the police for help. "Eavesdropping," I said. "But she couldn't very well tell Bryant about Marcel. Bryant would have welcomed a sale there. So she told him that Alice, working late, had seen him in the cloister just after he killed Hester. Then she enticed Alice to the office the night Alice surprised me so Bryant could silence her."

We went back down to the Abbaye, Cloudsmith's notebook crowded with his reporter's shorthand. When he wrote it all up, he handsomely gave me credit for my efforts and himself justly received an award for outstanding newswriting.

I had two other visitors before I left the Abbaye de Ste. Denise. The first was a thoroughly subdued Harry Charwood who came to thank me for saving his life. Poor Harry. I don't think he'd ever been indebted to anyone before, not that he'd admit anyway, and leastways to a woman.

José showed him out onto the terrace and he was uncharacteristically quiet, awkwardly rubbing his huge hands together. I put him at his ease as best I could and then asked him if his offer to lease John's unused acreage was still good. I knew before I did that I had him on the spot because with Grunnigen exposed, his blackmail revenue had to have been promptly cut off by Jaconello.

Of course, he tried to find excuses to extricate himself. I abruptly saved him the trouble by telling him I knew what he'd been up to. "It was a great scheme, Harry, using Jaconello's money to line your own pockets while appearing the man who saved John Seldridge's neck."

I was mostly bluff on my part. I had no actual proof of his blackmailing. His reaction, however, was proof enough. He was suitably stunned.

I took him off the hook. "Look, Harry," I said. "That's all strictly between you, me, and Jaconello who, I'm sure, will never say a word to anyone. He'd hardly want it known that someone had had him over a barrel."

Then I proposed he go right ahead with his offer.

"But I can't," he mumbled. "You know I haven't got that kind of money." He looked on fire with embarrassment.

"Yes, you do," I countered. "You have two sixteenth-century Flemish tapestries hanging in your living room. Together, they're surely worth the first three years rent. Your profit will pay the rest."

Almost at once, a surprised Harry reverted to his old self. "Those damned old rags of my mother?" he bellowed. "Why, I never. Dust collectors, that's all I thought they were."

José had brought out some champagne and we toasted a deal, and Harry's leasing John's unused acres turned out better than anyone could have imagined. What began as strictly business turned into a lucrative partnership and eventually a warm friendship.

My second visitor was, of course, Marcel Turbo. He arrived, as would be expected, on the front lawn in his helicopter, and I found myself having lunch with him once again, this time on his luxurious yacht as we cruised down San Francisco Bay.

He wanted to extend the cruise for the weekend, suggesting we head south along the coast for distant Santa Barbara. "There's a great restaurant there," he said, "and then I propose Tahiti."

It was an almost irresistible pitch. Almost. What woman

wouldn't have been tempted? Marcel was fun, fascinating, rich as Croesus, fabulously good-looking, and above all a really nice guy. And I was a single woman with few responsibilities except to myself.

Call it pride, if you wish, or self-esteem. Whatever, I didn't care to add myself to what I was certain had been an impressive number of predecessors enjoying similar yacht cruises.

Reluctantly, I said no.

And reluctantly, too, I finally said good-bye a few days later to the Abbaye de Ste. Denise winery and to John and Elissa.

It was late afternoon when I left. Shadows heralding yet another softly beautiful evening had stretched across the lawn. John had promised me a lifetime supply of his best wine and Elissa a visit the next summer to my home on Martha's Vineyard. José had beamed a farewell. They all stood in the doorway to wave as I drove away.

As I came opposite to the archway entrance to the cloister, I tried not to think of all the horror that had happened there. The old monastery buildings and the chapel looked so peaceful with their worn, sunbleached stone blocks, still partially covered with cracked adobe, here and there garnished by climbing wisteria and trumpet vine. Approaching the massive front gates, I reached without thinking for a transmitter to open them. But I had no need for one. The gates stood open.